D0848991

INSIDE THE WOLF

ALSO BY AMY ROWLAND

The Transcriptionist

INSIDE THE WOLF

a novel by

AMY ROWLAND

ALGONQUIN BOOKS OF CHAPEL HILL 2023

Published by
ALGONQUIN BOOKS OF CHAPEL HILL
Post Office Box 2225
Chapel Hill, North Carolina 27515-2225

an imprint of WORKMAN PUBLISHING CO., INC.
a subsidiary of HACHETTE BOOK GROUP, INC.
1290 Avenue of the Americas
New York, New York 10104

© 2023 by Amy Rowland. All rights reserved.
Printed in the United States of America.
Design by Steve Godwin.

This is a work of fiction. While, as in all fiction, the literary perceptions
and insights are based on experience, all names, characters, places, and
incidents either are products of the author's imagination or are used
ficticiously—including the fictional town of Shiloh, not intended to refer
to the actual town of Shiloh in North Carolina.

LIBRARY OF CONGRESS CATALOGING-IN-PUBLICATION DATA
Names: Rowland, Amy, [date]– author.
Title: Inside the wolf : a novel / by Amy Rowland.
Description: First edition. | Chapel Hill, North Carolina :
Algonquin Books of Chapel Hill, 2023. |
Summary: "After her academic career in New York flames out, Rachel
Ruskin returns to her family's tobacco farm in North Carolina and is
haunted by memories and by her hometown's buried history of racism
and violence. When a child is accidentally shot and killed, Rachel can no
longer avoid confronting her own past wrongs; nor can she continue to
hold herself apart from her community"— Provided by publisher.
Identifiers: LCCN 2023003913 | ISBN 9781643752716 (hardcover) |
ISBN 9781643755328 (ebook)
Subjects: LCGFT: Novels.
Classification: LCC PS3618.O877 I67 2023 |
DDC 813/.6—dc23/eng/20230202
LC record available at https://lccn.loc.gov/2023003913

10 9 8 7 6 5 4 3 2 1
First Edition

For Desmond

THE WOLF AND THE MASTIFF

A wolf, who was starved to the bone, met a sleek, strong mastiff. The wolf greeted the dog and commended him on his good looks. "You could easily get as fat as I am," said the mastiff. "How?" asked the wolf. "It's easy," said the dog. "Follow me." As they trotted along together, the wolf noticed a bald spot on the dog's neck. "What's that?" he asked. "Oh, it's nothing," answered the dog. "When I'm tied up, the collar rubs away a bit of fur." "Tied up!" cried the wolf. "You can't always run where you please?" "Not always," said the mastiff, "but I'm given such nice food and even sometimes a pat on the head. What does it matter that sometimes the master ties me up?" "It matters much to me," replied the wolf, and, though he felt weak with hunger, he ran full speed back to his home forest.

—AESOP

INSIDE THE WOLF

PART ONE

❦ ❦ ❦

STORY OF A SHOOTING

Early September 2015

ONE

I BURIED A wolf today. Last night's lightning downed the pin oak by the ditch, and the wolf must not have known to move in time. He was still lying there this morning, a reddish rug under the toppled trunk, grimacing with meat-tearing teeth. It's remarkably bad luck that he sheltered under the one tree felled by the storm. Perhaps he passed at the exact moment it hit the ground, but the odds of that seem even slimmer. I paused on my morning walk, bending to stroke his head, bony under the damp fur. Deciding where to wait it out is dangerous sometimes.

I buried him on the Old Place, where the stick barn used to stand. It collapsed into the ground years ago, and there's not a trace of the tar-papered barn, not a plank of sash-sawn wood. Without a trace, that's not true. A circle of dirt sits between the field and the woods as though swept clean. No grass grows in this spot, it's as barren as the Devil's Tramping Ground. The barn is gone, but the mind knows something was here.

The burial was hard work. I had to ferry the wolf across the yard in a wheelbarrow, and heave him onto the tarp in the truck bed. His grave is not deep, but it took all morning to dig. A strange first act as a farm owner. But I didn't want the body to attract all manner of scavengers. Besides, soon it would start to smell.

AFTER THE BURIAL, I walked the length of my family's land. It's mine now, but locals know that's only because my brother, Garland, died a year ago, and my parents finished themselves off in an accident this summer. It wasn't their fault, but I wonder if they didn't feel a flash of relief in that final moment before the collision. I don't know the odds of your entire family dying within a year. Maybe they're similar to those of sheltering under a doomed tree during a lightning storm.

Four Corners, it's called. The farm is a hundred acres square, with fields of corn, soybeans, and tobacco, surrounded by pinewoods on three sides. For twenty years, I've flown in for a day or two every six months and then torn back to New York as though chased by the devil. There are plenty of devils here, linking hands with history's ghosts. Some are harder to recognize than others. It's no wonder, my mother used to say, when Satan himself masquerades as an angel of light.

Once the wolf's bones are bare, I will dig him up and save his skull. I want to remember how light skulls can be. When I was a child, I kept a blue rabbit foot in my pocket. They were considered good luck charms, not gruesome souvenirs, but a talisman to keep evil away as we played in the dark. "Starlight, star bright, I hope to see a ghost tonight!" we sang, as we ran on the cool black grass. Little did we know one was already among us.

The skull is something to keep as a reminder, out in the open, not hidden away like my parents, who are currently resting in a shoebox under their own bed. They hated display of any kind.

Wolves are private, too, but I'm sure I saw this one last night. I was on the porch, drinking tea and listening to Agritalk radio (my new live-like-a-local project). It was just before dark when the wind picked up and the rain broke. Drops pocked the garden, then a rain wall pushed across the field toward the house. Lightning streaked the sky, and in a split second of illumination, I glimpsed the wolf through a clearing in the trees. The reddish fur made me think it was a coyote, though it's unusual to see them so near the house, as they, too, like to remain unseen. Maybe I was already spooked then, watching the storm, feeling how, for the first time, I was alone here, the nearest neighbor a quarter-mile away. *I'm being watched.* The hair rippled up my arms, and I chastised myself for feeling unnerved. *Starlight, star bright, I hope to see a ghost tonight!* The words came unwanted, unbidden, as the past pushed toward me like the rain wall. In the distance, lightning touched its electric branches to the trees below, and I went inside for candles and a flashlight in case the power went out. It was then that I heard the noise in the attic. I told myself squirrels had gotten in, but it wasn't that sort of sound. And today, I have buried a wolf, but I have not been up to the attic. I become immobile every time I think of climbing those narrow wooden stairs.

I WALK THE FARM, striking the ground with a stick, as my father did in the last years of his life. It's a landscape, flat and unforgiving, that invites striking. The field of tobacco is radiant in the late afternoon light; the plants glow softly, golden green, tough and pungent. Even now, I cannot say they are not beautiful. They stand sturdy and orderly, lined up like soldiers and just as lethal.

Why take so long to tell it? Why not lay it down in ink lines: Confess the family secret that weighs heavier after their deaths. I always told myself that teaching got in the way, that I was too busy turning my dissertation into a book to work on a more personal project. That's over now. In my tenure denial last spring, the committee said I was unable to make my studies on women, myth, and Southern folklore relevant for the "discipline." So here I am. There's no better place to live hidden among the pages of my life. I feel fear, and don't yet know whether I'm here for fruitful solitude or failure's refuge.

I lean my walking stick against the house and go inside, slamming the screen door now that my mother is no longer here to prevent it. Just after the slam, I hear the noise in the attic. It sounds like one shoe dropping.

I should investigate, but I can't. I stay downstairs, scribbling and striking through a To Do list:

DAY ONE:
Bury a wolf
Meet some chickens
Walk Four Corners
Clean out attic

I sit outside for an hour, waiting—for what, I don't know.

Dark, I guess. I don't want to face the old doors to the old rooms: my parents', Garland's, my own.

Maybe I've returned to see if the days are as long as I remember from the summer I was twelve. That was 1985, thirty years ago. Now it's five o'clock on a September day in Shiloh, North Carolina. Two tobacco fields flank the house, the plants green and deceptive as counterfeit. We were not to smoke. But sometimes we got sick from working with the leaves when they were wet with dew. Our parents called it tobacco sickness. We called it the green monster. It meant vomiting bile and a long day of hot misery. Because of that, and because it was gummy, sweaty back-busting work, I didn't like priming in the field. Hunching down the rows, breaking the bottom leaves off each plant. I didn't like driving the tractor either. I liked being at the barn where the women were looping the fat leaves and pounding gossip like dirt into dust. That's where the talk was, but I was not needed there. The wooden tobacco cart was hitched to the tractor, and I inched down the row as the primers fanned out behind me and disappeared into the deep green sea, only to rise and wade to the cart, dumping their bundles before turning and diving down again into the leafy waves. At the end of the day, when the barn was put in, I'd get twenty dollars cash. Once a week we'd drive to town and deposit it, or most of it, in my college fund. It was hard, long work that I approached with a mixture of dread and pride.

Every day, up a row, down a row, scooting to reach the clutch and sweating over the narrow turn at the end. Once, I swung the tobacco cart into the ditch, and nearly took the whole tractor in, too. I told my father I feared the end of each row, worrying I wouldn't make the tight turn.

"It will be fine if you don't fret, Rachel."

"But it happened once. It could happen again."

"Don't dwell," he said. "Everything is fine when you don't dwell."

He knew that everything was not fine. Something dreadful had happened, and each of us dwelled on it, in our own separate way.

I NEED OUT and there's only one place to go. The Bar, according to the neon sign, but known to everyone as Carl's Place, is a beat-up building, between a ranch house and the tiny post office on the main street. It's mostly residential; everything except beer and mail requires a trip to Greenvale twenty miles away.

A skinny boy with red hair and big feet is sitting on the steps, cradling a shotgun between his knees.

"Are you the bouncer?"

He doesn't respond, but swings his legs to the side so I can pass.

"It isn't loaded," he says glumly.

"That's good."

He blinks through his bangs. "Not good."

"Something needs shooting?"

"Just a target, an old scarecrow. But I can't do that unless an adult is with me," he says, responding sternly to my gently teasing tone.

"Safety first," I say. He rolls his eyes, and I resolve to try to be more kind. "I'm Rachel. Who are you?"

"Tom. I live over there." He points to the brick ranch house beside the bar.

"Someone knows you're here?"

"I'm allowed to sit here with my unloaded gun until mom calls me inside."

"See you around, Tom." I skirt his lanky legs and jog up the steps.

"Is it true you can start a fire by rubbing sticks together?"

"I can't, but someone can." I turn back to his pale face, freckled and familiar. "Do you want me to walk you home?"

"I live right there," he says sharply, and brushes my leg with the gun barrel as he points toward the house.

"Please be careful, Tom."

"It's not loaded!"

My life has been lived within the echo of those words. "That's good, but an unloaded gun is like a stick. It can still hurt someone."

"Sticks and stones may break my bones, but words can never hurt me."

If only that were true. I have a hard yearning for New York, where, confronted with a body on the stairs, you skirt it. Don't make eye contact. Don't initiate conversation. Brutal, but effective.

"Tom!" a woman's voice calls from the house. "Tom!"

He slides off the steps agile as a salamander and darts toward the shadowy outline of the house.

A rough-skinned man with a black headband looks at me sideways and nods to the bartender. He gestures to the stool beside him, and I have no choice but to sit. The forced politeness of small towns, where insisting on privacy is a snub that won't be forgotten by people you are bound to run into sooner or later, probably sooner.

He raises his wiry eyebrows at a short man sitting a few stools down, then smiles, revealing tobacco-tinted teeth. I order a gin and tonic from the bartender, who nods and goes about his task with quiet competence.

"A gin and tonic, I could tell you were high class," the man says. "Who are you?"

"Rachel Ruskin."

"A Ruskin. I see it, now you say it."

The short man, who has been sipping his beer slowly while studying his glass, says, "Don't mess with her, Ernest."

"I'm not messing. We're having a conversation."

The man nods. "Well, don't rush her off. Hard drinks should be drunk slow."

"That's Dennis, and I'm Ernest. We knew your dad from the hunting club. He was a stand-up man."

He strokes his temple as we watch the bartender bop down the bar for a rag.

"Back to settle affairs?" the bartender asks, returning and wiping the wood around the tap. "I heard you were selling the farm."

"I haven't decided whether to sell. Where'd you hear that?"

"I guess folks just assumed. Do you remember me? You were in my sister's class. Mary Boyd. I'm Billy."

He grins, and I see the ten-year-old brother of my best friend in middle school. After I transferred to Greenvale, our friendship faded.

"I was sorry to hear about your brother, and your parents, too. It was all so . . . sudden."

"Yes."

I'm the only one here with Billy and the barflies. The urge to flee rises like dust in my throat, but the tyranny of civility makes me stay put.

Ernest is talking about a red wolf shooting twenty miles away. The man who shot the wolf was arrested, and several people picketed the wildlife office with handmade signs.

"What will happen?" I ask, thinking of the body I buried this morning.

"If he's convicted it could mean a hundred grand and some months in jail. But that's unlikely."

"They can't prove he knew it was a wolf," Dennis says. "He thought it was a coyote."

"Is that what he's saying?"

"That's what he ought to say. Hell, it's hard for anybody to tell them apart. And now that they've interbred, and there are all kinds of hybrids running around, forget it. Even the professionals can't tell the difference. Coyotes and coywolves are about to swallow the whole state. They're everywhere now, bad as kudzu."

"Why are there so many?"

"There hasn't been a disease to clear them out in a while."

"How did they get here in the first place? I don't remember them being a problem when I was a kid."

"There's theories about that," Ernest says. "You want to hear them?"

"Oh, no," Dennis says. "Ernest is going to get theoretical with us."

"Don't pay him any mind," Ernest says. "He's just got PTSD, 'post-traumatic Southern disorder.'"

"Hell," Dennis says. "Everybody here's got that."

"He's sixty-two and lives with his mama. That's all you need to know."

"I'm going to move when she passes," Dennis says into his beer.

Billy winks to show that this is the oft-repeated play between two characters that might be waiting for God or Godot or mothers to die. It's also possible Billy the bartender is flirting, but I'm too old and not in the mood.

"So," Ernest says, "the first coyote theory, which I believe to be the least likely, is that Warrens introduced the wily creature."

"The lumber company?"

"The story, farfetched as it may be, is that they wanted to get rid of rabbits that were eating sap from their trees. You know they own millions of acres of trees around here. So they introduced the coyote, and accidentally gutted the deer population. Because coyotes will eat anything from Peter Rabbit to Bambi. But here's the problem, Rachel. Farmers rent their land to hunters. And guess what? No deer, no hunters, no fees."

Ah, corporate greed and self-interest, that well-worn storyline.

"Then you've got theory number two," Ernest says, holding up two knurled fingers, as Dennis nods and taps two fingers against his glass.

"Number two says those coyotes were just a-comin'. They had eaten up everything in the West and Midwest. They're adaptable, their population is exploding, and they're on the move. Why wouldn't they like it here? We've got good land, good eats, and good weather."

"Natural expansion, I'll buy that."

"Hold on. There's more. Now here's an unpopular one among the natives. That fox hunters brought them here. They put the foxes or coyotes in big pens, and release dogs to hunt them. It's good training, but sometimes the cunning coyote gets away."

Billy is refilling glasses, and I slide mine out of reach. He retrieves it and makes a second drink anyway. "On the house."

"Eat, drink, and be merry," Dennis says, lifting his glass. "For tomorrow we shall die."

"Shakespeare or Scripture?"

"Don't encourage him," Ernest says. "He's been watching too much Game of Thrones. Starting to talk like a telly. Now, back to the coyote-coywolf invasion. You've got your inevitable expansion. You've got Warrens. You've got some idiot foxhunters. And behind door number four is the government."

"Which they deny deny deny," Dennis adds.

"Some claim that when North Carolina reintroduced wild turkeys, they released coyotes to reduce the raccoons, who love to eat turkey eggs."

"Do you believe that?"

"As much as I like to blame the powers that be, the notion of the government keeping nature at bay is a bit much to my mind."

"Why do you think there are so many now, all of a sudden?"

"Look, they're ferocious. They eat everything in sight. And their predators and competitors: mountain lions, gone; wolves, almost gone; bears, outnumbered."

"Eat, drink, and be merry," Dennis repeats, lifting his glass, "for tomorrow, you never know."

We fall silent and sip our drinks. Dennis clears his throat and covers his mouth to swallow a burp. I feel obligated to continue the conversation, which is not and has never been my strong suit.

"There was a boy outside when I came in."

"Mr. Mopey with a shotgun? That's Tom. He's a good kid, lives next door. They moved in a year ago; the house was inherited."

Ernest's gaze takes in my face. "So, Leith and Linda's daughter. That was a sad business about your family."

"Ernest," Dennis interrupts. "Stop pestering her."

"I didn't mean any harm. It's hard when it's sudden like that." Dennis raises his hand in warning, but Ernest continues. "I'm dying myself, it's just taking a while. I've been poisoned with pesticides. It's a slow poison, giving me time to ease into the idea and say my good-byes. It's a hell of a contradiction ain't it, these good Christian farmers killing us slowly."

"It could have been Agent Orange," Dennis says quietly. "Could have been cigarettes."

"Could have been," Ernest agrees. "And I didn't mean any insult to your family about farming, Rachel. I know about containing contradictions. I was in Vietnam," he says, looking at me. "Killed more men than I could name or number. On purpose, I guess, at the time. Haunts the hell out of me now, witnessing all that death. I saw my best buddy shoot himself in the face when his rifle jammed."

He strokes his headband and cups his sweaty glass.

"Ernest, you know that wasn't a mishap," Dennis says.

"It was."

This is another argument they must take up like the nightly knitting. I leave my drink and walk out into the warm air.

On the short drive home—it's too dark to walk—I remember Billy's freckled face exactly as it was when his sister and I were friends. We had bonded over word pockets and lemon twists in Ms. Beasly's first-grade class. Ms. Beasly had black hair piled high, and I was mesmerized when she scratched her head with a pencil and it disappeared into the dark hive. She wore wrap dresses, drove a green MG, and was the most glamorous creature I had ever seen. I lived for her story hour, and on the day of our Halloween party, she read from a book of North Carolina ghost stories.

The story was about a Witch Bride, who slips out of her skin at night and flies into the dark, returning to her body at dawn. I was dying to know where she went and what she did and what it felt like to fly. But it was not the Witch Bride's story—it was her husband's. One night, he discovers her adventures in the dark, and rubs red pepper all over his wife's abandoned suit of flesh. When she returns at daylight and slips back into her skin, the pepper tortures her. She rolls and tumbles and takes "gravely ill," dying later the same day. Upon hearing this, I sobbed. Pepper in your skin! Ms. Beasly took me aside and told me it was fine that the husband killed her, because she was a witch.

"But you're a witch," I said to Ms. Beasly, pointing to her black hat. She was wearing a witch costume for our class party.

"Only today," she said. "And I'm a good witch."

That's how it was here, from witches to wolves: calling something evil to justify its killing. Southerners, even more than most, have clung to their imagined villains. As a folklore scholar in grad school, I had begun my dissertation with the cautionary tale of the Witch Bride. It is her metamorphosis that allows her freedom, which is always fleeting.

TWO

I TURN OFF the road and the headlights catch a figure in the driveway. It's Tobias, the neighboring farmer. My father has been renting land to him for years, and he's always eager for another acre.

He lifts his hand against the glare, wiping his forehead with his baseball cap before replacing it with a casual, exaggerated slowness.

"It's good to see you, Rachel."

My face flushes, and I come around to the front of the car, grateful we're only partially visible in the headlights. He taps the gravel drive with his steel-toe boot and looks at me with his wide, toothsome smile. He has always had a look of lightly controlled impulse, which some women find irresistible. I was one of them myself once.

"I saw you earlier, inspecting the land. Seeing how I've managed it?"

"You're a solid farmer, Tobias. I know that."

"It's in my blood."

"Crops care about water and weather, not about blood."

"We were lucky this year." He steps toward me in the darkness and gestures toward the field, which gives off the unmistakable scent of tobacco. It smells sweetest at night, jasmine with a hint of tea leaf. "People thought your dad was crazy to keep farming tobacco after the government buyout got rid of subsidies, but it's going to work out okay this year. I'll take it to auction later this fall, and next year we'll rotate corn and soybeans." He adds quickly, "If you agree and want to keep renting. We could talk about a sale, too. How long are you home?"

"Maybe I'll stay."

He laughs dismissively. "You haven't lived here in over twenty years, New York. How are you?"

I've got no job and no family, I think but don't say. There is only one response here. "Can't complain."

I don't ask how he is because I don't want to make it easy for him, and because I have a pretty good idea of what his life is like through all the seasons, the sowing, the harvesting, the curing, the work in the fields, the steel-toed boots, eating a squishy sandwich with dirty hands on lunch break, beers at night, a game of pool here or there, hunting season, the baying of the dogs, the ritual of the kill.

"I remember your hair like that," he says, "all falling down."

I have pulled part of it back in a clip and left the ends hanging, in a way I have not worn in years. He touches the short sleeve of my dress, a floral one I found in the cedar chest.

"I remember all of it."

Tobias is not the only man I've known with trapper eyes and rough hands. Some hide it better, but I can't call Tobias deceptive. He wears his wants on his face.

"That was a long time ago."

"Time doesn't happen here, New York. Aren't you going to invite me inside?"

"What happened to your wife?"

"She liked the idea of country life but not the living of it. She's in a Greenvale subdivision with a pink-face banker. No kids at least, so that's good."

"Tobias, I know you're anxious to buy the land, but I haven't made any decisions yet."

"You're thinking of staying, even better. We can be partners. Farmers can't make it alone here."

"You seem to."

"I get by, but I'm a part-time farmer and a full-time mechanic. If it's not the tiller or the sprayer or the combine that needs work, it's one of the tractors. We used to have migrants and now we have machines. I run the farm on community college classes and YouTube videos."

I'd noticed the hulking metal heaps on my way into town. There used to be a seasonal labor camp a few miles west, with barbecue pits and scattered trailers. Now it's a graveyard or body shop for farm equipment. The words DIOS ESTÁ AQUÍ are still visible on one of the broken trailer doors, under a partially collapsed roof.

"Eva at the post office says it's just you and a bunch of books, a boatload, enough to start a library." He reaches for my shoulder and I shrug him off. "How old are you now, Rachel, forty-one?"

"Forty-two," I correct him, "a perfect number."

"Actually it's a primary pseudoperfect number," he says airily.

"It was a manner of speaking," I retort, though my face is hot.

His calloused knuckle grazes my cheek and the car headlights illuminate his lupine smile. "You can only play farmer for a little while before it gets hard. Winter's coming; maybe a drought, maybe a flood."

"Good night, Tobias."

"Call me if you want company. Or if you're afraid."

"I'm not afraid."

"You've never lived alone here. It's dark as the back of beyond. The coyotes make such a racket it sounds like you're surrounded."

"I'll be fine. I don't think coyotes will blow the house down."

He looks at the house, a looming white shape that can't be fully covered with darkness.

"I think it was a wolf," Tobias says, "and he came down the chimney."

"Yes, and the pig made a fire and cooked him for dinner."

"I guess there are different versions."

"There always are."

I wait for him to leave as I turn toward the house, filled with foreboding. I grew up here, but I always thought of this as my parents' house, where they lived from marriage until death. It had been vacant and converted to a workspace for a decade before they reclaimed it. My mother said the first time she saw it they were slaughtering pigs in the living room, and she could hear them crying as they waited their turn.

I AWAKEN ON the couch with *Ghosts of the Carolinas* on my face. It's past midnight. Somewhere in the woods coyotes are yipping, a long eerie bark with a hint of laughter. I step outside, into the tar dark. It's as though I don't exist in it, or as if I exist as an unseen ghost. It could be anything, or nothing, out there, a tunnel or a tomb or the sea floor. New York is another country. That's where I was when Garland died, consumed with a love affair and my stupid little life. I was leaving a Eugene O'Neill play when the sheriff called.

My brother sat on a downed dogwood, with its petals in the shape of the cross. He took out his phone and made a call. When the sheriff told me this, I felt my body relax because it couldn't be true that Garland was dead. He was on the phone. He was calling someone. Maybe it was me. I had to get off the phone in case he was trying to reach me.

"Then he took the .36 Glock from his jacket and shot himself," the sheriff said. Garland had been calling with directions to his body so his organs could be donated. They salvaged his blood, his liver, and took skin, bone, tendons, and corneas.

"What do you mean salvaged?" I cried. "It's already done?"

"It's already done."

"What are you saying?" I repeated, waiting for the words to make sense. "He's been harvested?"

"So to speak," the sheriff said. "I told your parents I'd call. They're not able to talk just now."

The play I had just seen was a lauded production of *Long Day's Journey into Night*. My theater date was Lucas, the sociologist I was adulterating with. He was separated, making it both safe and sanctioned. I sat stiff and resistant in the first act, almost offended at O'Neill's long-windedness, as failure, shame, and morphine contribute to a family's slow-motion collapse over the course of a day. The youngest son, whose character I hadn't even liked, had spoken about being at sea and feeling a part of it, and yet feeling a ghost, and thinking how wrong that he had been born human and should have been a seagull. He would always be a stranger who never felt at home. I had bewildered myself by crying at this notion of being born the wrong animal, and the silent tears continued as I thought of the inexpressible in all the bodies, the actors and the audience sitting in the dark with synced heartbeats, and the morphine-addled mother on stage saying again and again how we can't help what life has done to us. But we can, I wanted to shout, knowing I doubted, though I wanted to believe. I was embarrassed at weeping over O'Neill, and Lucas was embarrassed, too. We had left the theater with distance between us, our bodies separate as we swam up to the surface of life after being submerged in the black box. I was over-whelmed with sadness at how we're all trapped in our own skin, and thinking how wrong that I was born a human and should have been born a—but I came up blank. When I saw my parents' area code on my phone, I felt a sense of doom even before answering.

I flew to North Carolina for Garland's funeral, of which I have almost no memory. The things I recall are random—sitting on the plane beside a man who needed a seatbelt extender, standing in line at the rental car counter, passing the sign for the Country Doctor's Museum in Bailey, needing a bathroom badly forty miles from Shiloh, and deciding to hold it. Nine months later I flew back again to collect my parents' ashes and stash them under their bed. Through lawyers, I arranged for Tobias to rent the farm and finish the season. I vamoosed to New York. On returning, I found that mice had moved into my Morningside apartment. I was only away four days, I protested to an amused exterminator, who stomped two mice with his boots as we talked, and covered the pipe under the sink with steel wool. Then I cleaned tiny baby mice out of the sink drain, where they nestled with their eyes sealed closed and their dead hand-like paws tucked under their chins. My career was over, so when my lease ended around Labor Day, I put everything in storage and flew back south. I don't have to stay, I told myself. I can leave anytime.

I SET ASIDE the ghost book and walk through the rooms of my parents' house. At Garland's door, I almost knock, as he trained me in childhood. *Knock, knock! Who's there? Fred. Fred who? Who's a Fred of the big bad wolf?* Garland would open the door and say, "That's so bad you must have made it up yourself. Come in if you got to, Nerd Biscuit."

"Why thank you, Turd Blossom."

Then he would let me demolish him in gin rummy.

On his dresser, the worn blue rabbit foot that we passed back and forth lies severed and alone. It shocks me now, how I loved to touch it in my pocket, never connecting it to the wild freedom of rabbits I sometimes saw from a distance, eating fallen fruit from the pear tree or the blueberry bush. Next to the foot, change is stacked by size, quarter to penny, neat and undisturbed as rocks. A snake's rattlers rest at the bottom of an old coffee can, among shotgun shells and forgotten paper slips, including his hunting license. My father bought him (but not me, the girl) a lifetime license when he was a year old: "It's cheaper that way." If Garland hadn't taken his license when he moved out, he must have been looking for a whole new life. He wasn't much of a hunter, but he went along. He did what was expected of him, until he cut us off.

He moved in with Jewel and was taking engineering courses at the community college while he worked night shifts at the spinning mill. Some of his old shoes are in the closet, chukka boots, shabby slippers, dingy Converses. Hanging between his old flannel robe and his letter jacket is the small green coat that belonged to our childhood friend. Rufus Swain, the minister's son, "Professor" we called him. Given how Professor died, Garland wasn't able to wear the hand-me-down, and it has hung in the closet all these years. Professor loved that corduroy coat more than anything. It was too big for him, and thread hung from one of the loose brown buttons that were fat and latticed across the top. After the funeral, Minister Swain had given it to Garland. I remember clearly when he came to the house. We watched from the window as he crossed the yard, carrying the folded coat in his outstretched arms like a lamb, the sleeves hanging down like little legs.

THREE

IN THE MORNING I find myself on the road to the Swains' house, determined to return Professor's coat. I grip the steering wheel tight as I approach Spivey's Crossroads. *Lift your feet up over the railroad tracks, or break your mama's back,* Garland, Professor, and I used to warn, riding our bikes on this country road, slapping one another's bug-bitten legs. I lift my feet despite myself, as though they rise of their own accord. The fields flicker past. I had been desperate to leave this place with my scholarship, to take refuge in the green oak and red-brick of my college campus, far from these bleached skies and sunbaked dust.

The dignified lonely house perches atop an incline, detached from woods and field, almost from the land itself. Professor's mother is taking laundry off the line. She's gaunt, her narrow face ravaged.

"Roberta," I say, going in for the hug. That's how it's done here. No point fighting it. A brief look of confusion crosses her face, and I wince, letting go of decades of women's studies. "Miss Roberta."

She brightens, and I feel her bones through the embrace.

"Come in, Rachel," she says, touching her elegant bun of gray-brown hair and ushering me inside.

The kitchen smells of tomatoes, which sit in mounds like flavored stones on the counter.

"I've got to can, but Jefferson wants me to wait until he gets home from his office at the church. I tell him he's a minister who keeps banker's hours. He's being over cautious, but it's true I'm a little forgetful these days."

I carry Professor's coat, and she watches it closely, but makes no move to take it. Instead she serves coffee and chocolate layer cake. "It's never too early when you have a visitor." I eat carefully, with the jacket lying awkwardly across my lap.

"You've been away so long, Rachel. I was terribly sorry about your parents and Garland, too."

Her sincerity punctures my defenses. I glimpse the moment of impact when my parents crashed, when the bullet entered Garland's brain, and shudder.

Roberta must notice, and she says kindly, "It's nice of you to drop by. Is something on your mind?"

Last night I dreamt I was like the sister in the wild swans tale, who must knit nettles into shirts so that her brothers, changed into birds by an evil witch, can return to human form. In the fairy-tale logic of sleep, I had spun Professor's coat of lamb's wool to turn him back into a live boy. I hadn't finished the second sleeve when he took it from me, and so he was doomed to be a boy with one arm and one lamb leg. I can't tell Roberta that, but I awoke gripped with a conviction:

I have to tell her the truth about what happened that terrible night.

"I'd like to talk to you about Professor—Rufus. Is that all right? I've brought his jacket. It belongs to you."

She reaches out, then pulls her hand back. "I see him so clearly in his corduroy coat. I see you at his age, too. You were such a headstrong girl."

"You mean bossy."

"You were a handful. And Rufus was so agreeable, wasn't he? He was in awe of you."

"He was wonderful."

"Yes," she says, covering one hand with the other, and I think of a bird, an ortolan. They've been in the news recently, a story about French chefs trying to get the ban overturned. The tiny creatures are fattened up and then drowned in Armagnac. Diners cover their heads in napkins and eat the birds whole. Something about hiding from God. Or maybe they don't want other diners to see them spit out a bone or a beak. "Yes," she repeats. "He was a wonderful boy."

I don't know how to tell her what I've come to say. I start to speak, but she grips my wrists.

"It was a horrible accident," she says, almost a warning.

I place the jacket on her lap, and kneel before her. "I'm so very sorry."

"I know," she says, holding my hand on her knee. "But, you see, I believe his death was fated by God. What happens is His will. It's hard medicine, true enough. It must be harder for you."

"Why?"

"For a nonbeliever it's harder. Not the loss. I was his mother, after all. There is nothing worse than the death of a child, nothing on this earth. But for those without faith, there's no comfort. Your mother harbored hope for your soul, Rachel. We talked about you sometimes."

She looks at me with troubled copper brown eyes. She was kind when we were young, not caustic or impatient like some of the mothers whose hands were always itching to discipline any child close enough to catch.

"I'm not judging you, Rachel. I've struggled with God myself."

This surprises me—both the doubt and the admission—but I forge ahead.

"Roberta, I want to talk to you about the night of Professor's death."

"But why? It was an accident. I can't bear any more than that."

"Roberta, please—"

"There's something I never told Jefferson," she says, her voice quickening. "I've been thinking about it a lot lately. It was on Rufus's birthday, the year he died. I was alone. Jefferson and I had spent the evening together. I told him to go to his office and work on his sermon. We had grieved together, but we needed to grieve apart. So he went, and it became quite late. I couldn't sleep. I had put my knitting and reading aside. I couldn't settle on anything. There's no other way to say this, Rachel. I felt a presence in the house. Then I heard a noise in the attic, so I went to investigate. When I flipped the switch at the bottom of the stairs, the light didn't come on. I thought the bulb had burnt out, so I got a new one and went up in the dark. As I neared the top of the stairs, I heard Rufus."

She is squeezing my hand hard, and I get off my knees and move to the chair.

"I am telling you, Rachel, and I will tell God or anybody because it is the truth. Rufus was there. I couldn't see him, but he was calling me. *Mama. Mama.* I was shaking and crying, *Rufus. My son!* And he said, It's okay, Mama. I'm here. I'm with Joe Brooks. We're looking for his head."

Joe Brooks was the Black man who was supposedly decapitated by a train in 1939. We were trying to get a glimpse of his ghost the night Professor died. We wanted to claim that we, too, had seen his lantern moving along the tracks, as Joe searched for his head.

"I know how it sounds, but that's what happened."

We never told anyone we were looking for Joe Brooks that night. Roberta and I are sitting knee to knee, and goosebumps sprout along my arms.

"I had them too, Rachel. I have them now," and she touches her frail forearms. "At first, I was beside myself. Looking all around the attic and telling Rufus to come home or tell me where he was and I'd come get him. He said, No, no, mama. I can't come home. I was crying and carrying on, and he was being so gentle. That's how Rufus was. He wanted me to know he was safe."

"You never told Jefferson?"

"I couldn't. I was distraught. I sat in the attic and sobbed. Then I felt Rufus's presence around me, and I felt peaceful for the first time since his death. You can't tell folks around here these things. They might think you are defying God. 'Let no one be found among you who consults the dead.' Deuteronomy, I think. I was going to tell Jefferson right away. I went downstairs and picked up the phone. Then I heard his car in the drive. He could see I'd been crying, and he put his arms around me. Right there," she says, pointing to the door. "And I couldn't tell him. He might think I was going crazy. I couldn't stand to be doubted. I know it was Rufus. It wasn't a voice in a dream. It was his voice, *his voice*, in the room with me. It was my son.

"I was going to tell Jefferson the next day, then the next. Then too much time had gone by. I miss Rufus every day of my life, but I know he is at peace. He was such a sweet and helpful boy. He's helping me now, to face this disease."

"Are you sick, Roberta?"

She leans toward me and I'm struck by the straightforwardness in her look, the touch of grimness around her mouth. She's always been spare, and I had assumed the hollows under her cheeks and eyes were from age.

"It's called Pick's, that's the name of it, because it picks holes in your brain."

"Roberta," I say, unable to hide my horror. "I'm so sorry."

"I'm not. It's possible I'll become delusional and forget that Rufus is dead. Won't that be wonderful? It will be like he's alive. I would give him anything, even my mind."

The prickles spread to my scalp, and I feel the old panic I associate with the women of Shiloh: the Mothers. They terrified me, these women of my mother and Roberta's generation, who were crowded out of their own selves by motherhood. First they became mothers to their children, then their husbands, then the community.

It became their one and only role, made frightening because the very thing they were lauded for, respected for, valued for, was the same thing that destroyed their selfhood.

"Are you okay, Rachel? You're turning red."

"I have to go," I say, and rush toward the door, leaving the jacket crumpled on the chair. I can't tell her now.

As I'm crossing the porch, she says, from behind the screen door, "Have you been to see him?"

I turn back, and have a flash of Lot's wife turning to salt. I don't want to look back. I want to flee this place. And yet, I can't help it. The screen is like a veil obscuring her face, the wrinkles softened, her high cheekbones more pronounced, and I see her as she was when we were children. Soft-spoken, kind and patient, helping Professor and me make Easter kites or corn shuck dolls, always baking, letting Professor and me lick the chocolate frosting pan.

"To see him?"

"His grave. It's a nice spot your family gave him. It gives me peace."

I drive away, shaken. Roberta would sacrifice anything for her son. The thought of giving up your mind to live in memory terrifies me, but I know she would do it. I think of the folktale about a dead child who appears to his grief-stricken mother. He is crawling behind a group of free and radiant children, but his clothes are so weighed down with his mother's tears that he fears he will drown.

AT A CURVE before the crossroads, I pass the place where, one Sunday, Garland chased a deer. He had just gotten his license and was driving us home from church when, without a word, he pulled over, jumped out of the car, and sprinted into the woods without closing the door. We could see flashes of his gray suit jacket as he ran among the leafless winter trees in his stiff wingtips, his red tie flapping over his shoulder. Who knows what made him stop at a place we passed every day, where we saw deer more often than not? He could be like that, ready to race, to run full tilt. But he wasn't chasing the deer. He was fleeing us, fleeing time, fleeing that night in 1985, when three of us went into the woods and two came out and agreed to live by a lie.

My palms sweat as I near the railroad tracks. I try to distract myself. (*Think happy thoughts*, my mother used to say when I had nightmares as a child. *Think happy thoughts*.) I lift my feet over the tracks, and then it is passed. I am past.

I DRIVE BY a cornfield, then a copse of pines, green needles against a greener shade, and the memory of Garland fades into the rearview mirror just as a white figure darts across the road. My foot flashes to the brake, and I feel a soft thump as my head dips toward the steering wheel.

The road is empty. I scramble from the car, and feeling along the front grill, I touch a clump of snowy hair edged in blood. I jog over to the ditch, and slide down, but find nothing.

"Why did you run in front of me?" I ask the air.

I should try to find the animal and put it out of its misery. But I'm kidding myself that I could follow through with it. Hunters call these crippling losses, when an animal is wounded and escapes into the woods. Sometimes the wounded survive, but often, they elude their trackers and die maimed and alone. I lean back in the ditch, immobile, blinking up at the sun, like, I can't help thinking, Flannery O'Connor's grandmother after the Misfit shoots her. "Maybe they put you in by mistake," she says to the escaped convict. "It wasn't no mistake," the Misfit says.

A face appears above me. It's Palmer Brooks, Joe Brooks's son, an old man himself now.

"You alright down there?"

"I hit something."

"What was it?"

"Probably a deer." I'm not sure it was a deer at all. A dog? Too tall. And there's the spectral body I barely glimpsed as it flew in front of the car. It could have been a white deer. Hunters have supposedly seen them on rare occasions, but I never have.

"Well, you can't help him now." He holds out his hands to pull me up. "You better move your car out of that curve. Someone might not see."

He reaches closer and his hands float above me. They are strong and lined with time, work and wear and cold and heat, sun and wind, worn from gathering and mending and repairing. He and dad bonded over frugality and making old things work again. After they had fixed mom's oven for the final time, they took it to the dump and sold it for scrap, so Dad wouldn't have to pay to have it carted off when the new oven came.

"Why didn't I stop sooner, Palmer?"

"It happens," he says, tightening his grip and pulling me to my feet. "They've learned a lot, but not when to cross the road."

"They don't have a chance."

I'm shaking and have the terrible feeling I might cry. Palmer takes me by the elbow and repeats that I'm all right, that it happens, that there's nothing you can do when they run in front of you.

I pull the car onto the shoulder, and Palmer and I walk the yellow line. I keep hearing the sick thump, and almost feel the black cord of road spooling from my gut.

"My father would say I was driving too fast."

"He was a cautious man. Though if you had been a little faster, you would have already been by here when the deer crossed."

We half-laugh, and the leaves flutter above, showing their silvery undersides like little fishes. It's as though the two of us are walking the bottom of a deep deep water under the swimming things. I want to ask Palmer about ghosts and about his father, Joe, but I don't know how to start.

"Rachel, I was sorry about your folks."

"Thank you."

"Have you seen Jewel?"

"No. Garland and I weren't speaking much the last few years."

"You knew they were together?"

Garland and I had grown even more distant before his death. He always made an excuse not to see me when I visited and I didn't push. My mother told me—when was it, a couple of years ago?—that Garland was seeing Palmer's granddaughter. It's telling that she identified Jewel as Palmer's, because we knew other members of the family, too, but Palmer was everyone's marker. Community memories were tied to the summer Palmer saved a child from a cottonmouth, or the winter Palmer was found in the Baseline ditch, snake-bitten himself, and half frozen to death.

"Yes, but I never knew Jewel very well. I didn't know if she'd want to hear from me."

"Our families have known each other a long time," he says. "And now we have our beautiful Lyric."

"Who's Lyric?"

"Your niece."

"I don't have a niece."

"You do. Jewel had a baby eight months ago. She wasn't showing at Garland's funeral. She didn't want to tell your family. Said your parents had never shown any interest in her and she didn't want them to feel obligated. Jewel is not one to be beholden."

"I'd love to meet my niece."

"You get used to the idea first," Palmer says. "You're not rushing off anywhere, are you?"

"Would Jewel see me?"

"Take your time. They're not leaving. Are you?"

I toss the unanswered question in the air as we turn off the blacktop onto a shady lane that leads to the town baseball field.

"Did you ever think of leaving, Palmer?"

"I can't go. People think my father is a ghost story, and I'm here to remind them he was a man. They say he is a ghost who walks the tracks looking for his head. They say he was a caboose man killed in an accident, and that's a lie."

That was the story I learned as a child, that Joe Brooks was in the caboose when it broke loose and collided with an oncoming passenger train. I learned years later that wasn't at all what happened to Joe Brooks. His body was mutilated, but not by a train. Many people were present, but they were not passengers.

"My father, Joe, was a Pullman in the Brotherhood of Sleeping Car Porters. Caboose man," he scoffs. "That's a lie they repeated and printed on paper in that book of ghost stories. He was a Pullman. Handsome in a way people took note of. That's what my mother told me, so I have to believe it. He knew she was pregnant when he died. She did cling to that, but I don't know which way is worse. Seems like it just gave him more to worry about."

There are so many questions, but I can't bring myself to ask. A couple of years ago, one of my students asked, How do you know when a story is your story? I made up some tepid nonsense about writing the story you can't let go of, with respect. That's why I study folklore, I had clumsily explained. Our folk tales and ghost stories are the way we instruct, the way we warn, the way we choose to remember—or forget— our history of violence.

"I walk it out," Palmer says. "For me, walking is louder than talking. Everybody sees me. People act like they don't know things. That's the deal. That's the way we do here. But everybody knows."

I ask Palmer if he believes in ghosts.

"If you're going to live in a haunted place, you may as well believe in haunts."

FOUR

THE OVERGROWN GARDEN, a tufty patch in the backyard, accuses with its weedy neglect. I haven't had the heart to work in my mother's beloved vegetable garden. In the summer months she was out with the dew. In winter, she would slip into her green plastic boots and come back with huge heads of cabbage and collards, cut with the pearl-handled knife that Garland had made for her. There are dents and dirt holes now, where deer and rabbits and rodents have helped themselves to the spoils. They are eating my mother's life's work, which I both resent and appreciate.

Something has to be done. I grab gloves and head toward the wild watermelon vines spilling across the rows and into the grass. Before I've weeded a complete row, Tobias pulls up. He's with the boy from the bar, Tom. They come to the edge of the garden, standing together, one pale and scrawny, one tall and tan.

"We brought you something," Tom says. "It's a dog."

"Don't need a dog."

"June," Tobias says. "She was your dad's."

"Junebug? I thought he sold her."

"He did, but the new owner brought her back. He said she doesn't like hunting. She wants to be a yard dog."

"I didn't know."

"He didn't want a pet. Said she wouldn't chase anything but her own tail or a buttermilk biscuit."

"Thanks for taking her in."

"I had to. Everybody here wants a hunting dog or a yard dog, but not a yard dog that failed as a hunting dog. Anyway, she likes Tom. They get on fine."

"If you want to keep her, Tom, I'll sell her for a handshake."

"She's your dog," he says, looking at the ground.

"His mom says she doesn't need anything else that eats. But I told Tom you would let him visit."

"Anytime."

He asks Tom to bring June from the truck and we watch him cross the yard, dragging his big bare feet through the cool grass.

"Rachel, don't you have a job Tom could do? Something to keep him busy after school, before his mom gets home from work?"

"I don't have anything."

"He could mow the grass or help with the garden."

"No, Tobias. Why are you pushing this?"

"The kid's bored. I thought maybe you could help."

"I can't. Why are you so attached?"

"He showed up at the barn one day, and he hangs around, looking for something to do, ways to help out. He's a good kid, but he's lonely as hell."

Tom brings June over. She is on a short leash and looks rather embarrassed about the situation. June is a redbone, with a delicate head, long ears, light red-rimmed eyes, and fur resembling a red wolf's but a deeper shade, closer to Carolina clay.

"Come see her whenever you like, Tom."

He nods, dejected. June is restless, and she pushes her nose against his pocket, seeking treats. He pulls out two crumbly biscuits.

"You ever had a dog, Tom?"

"No."

"Neither have I. My dad had them, but they were hunting dogs, not really pets."

"Well, June's a pet," Tobias says. "No doubt about that. She's no working dog."

JUNE IS PAWING at the door by the time I get my shoes, so I sit outside on the steps to put them on as she licks my face.

"You're a yard dog, got it?"

Off the leash, she races, fast and low to the ground, like a ferret I once saw when apartment hunting in New York. "Don't worry about him," the woman subletting her place had said. "I'll take him with me. He just likes to run around." The crazed creature raced around and around the room, a New York story wrapped around a New York metaphor. I lose sight of June and worry she's run off. But if she does, someone will return her. Everyone here knows exactly what belongs to you.

Down a dirt path between two tobacco fields, the old oak waits alone and apart, watching over seven stubby headstones. The cemetery can't be seen from the road, and though the oak towers above the tobacco plants, the graves can only be found if you walk to the back of the field and look for them, know to look for them.

I let myself in through the creaky gate. No one here cares about keeping anyone out, and even the most superstitious aren't concerned that those within its confines will escape, but it's a state law that a family cemetery on private land be enclosed by a gate.

The headstone:

RUFUS "PROFESSOR" SWAIN
1974–1985
Blessed are the pure in heart,
for they shall see God.

Someone has been here recently. The grass is mowed; the area around the headstone is trim and tidy. It must be Minister Swain. He asked my father permission for this plot. It was probably for proximity; the Swains visited the grave often. It was hard not to see a tint of revenge in the request. Sometimes we saw their car passing, going to, going from. The tension came not from the grave itself, but from who would tend it. My father would go out to mow with the tractor, and Minister Swain would send him away. When my father said gruffly that it was his land after all, and his responsibility, Minister Swain replied that it was his son, and he would care for him. He noted, with what might have been ministerial authority and might have been fatherly anger, that duty to kith and kin was above that even to the land. It was years later that my parents chose cremation for themselves, which is still an uncommon choice here.

June has found me. She licks my ear then goes off to explore, while I kneel in the grass beside the grave.

THE DAY OF Professor's funeral was humid and hot. My parents argued over whether we should go. Garland and I were both heart plowed, but we banded together and begged. That was how we heard Minister Swain give the service for his own son. Everyone stared at us, especially at Garland. It was the first time I noticed how much he looked like our father, with those same light green eyes like sun-bleached pine needles.

Professor was at the front of the church alone. A different, a separate stillness enveloped him, and I stood in the aisle staring until my mother guided me firmly to our pew. The casket was open, and the sound of singing came as from far away. "In the Sweet By and By." That's Professor. That was Professor. I was upset with the tenses—*we shall meet on that beautiful shore*—and I wanted to touch him, but he was so stiff, his jaw so rigid, that I looked down at my tight patent shoes. The button eyes looked back at me. They were not my friends.

We filed out of church and drove to the family cemetery at the edge of the field, leaving the cars along the dusty shoulder and walking the path to the place with half a dozen headstones gray as November skies. We stood in the heat by the open grave, under the old oak and the lone cypress. Minister Swain said, "There will be no more tears—*there*." Those are the only words I remember. Where is the *there*? I wanted to know. I was already beginning to worry that, like Big Beech Island, which was not an island but a beech patch in the woods, heaven was not all that its name promised. After, while I was still shocked that the church elders and deacons were shoveling dirt on

Professor, my father, who was a deacon himself, reached out
to steady the minister. He had stepped close to the edge of the
burial pit when the coffin was lowered in with ropes. I had
seen these large men climbing to hang tobacco in barns, and
I had seen them bent over tractor engines and chicken eggs.
They were used to doing things alone, and though they were
strong, it took effort for them to move in unison.

As Professor disappeared into the ground, I heard a thump
from behind. Garland was kicking a cypress knee. I went
to him and we kicked the stump, first him, then me, then
Garland again. His face was red and he lifted his eyes to mine
as he swung his leg forward. His foot landed on my shin. The
pain was so sharp I inhaled in surprise. He kicked me again.
I kicked him back. The funeral goers were staring at us, with
the pursed-lip disapproval I knew so well. We kicked each
other with steady, concentrated blows, just as we had been
kicking the cypress, taking turns in quiet concentration, until
my father jerked us apart. That's how we left Professor; my
father's large hands gripping our necks, leading us away from
the grave, as the town of mourners followed.

JUNE BARKS, startling me back to the present, where I find
myself lying in the grass, under a low sky, halved by a hairline
crack of pink. In the breeze so slight it is barely a breeze comes
a smell of sulfur and stagnation. Across the western pond,
pines edge the banks, reflected murkily on the still surface.
The trees in the water are mottled with algae and green dust.
It is shocking that this smelly pond was once dark and glassy,
a spot for frogging and for sulking alone when troubled. June
sniffs at the edge, but I pull her back and turn toward home.

AT THE HOUSE, I look over my list, which is turning into the doodlings of a madwoman. On either side are slanted lines with random notes—books to order, names of people to write to in New York, most of whom I hadn't told I was leaving. There's even my poor sketch of a wolf alongside fragments of what threatens to become a fictional project, about Virginia Dare, the Witch Bride, and a feral girl resembling my childhood self.

I chastise myself as I make dinner, fighting a sense of unease. This is where I grew up. Nothing to be frightened of. Don't indulge in overfed fooleries, my mother used to say. Of course I'm unsettled, after losing my entire family within a year. And there is the lesser grief of being fired and feeling a failure, all the more because I tried to write folklore into academic literature.

There's also the fresher unease of my conversation with Roberta. It has tapped my discomfort with motherhood as I witnessed it growing up, and also the apprehension of some inexplicable being in the attic. The irrationality of this doesn't banish foggy notions that my family is being punished for our lie. That the ghost in the attic, even if it does not *really* exist, is the reminder that I alone must live out the sentence.

After an omelet, I lie down with the legend of Virginia Dare the White Doe. The Witch Bride aroused my imagination, but Virginia Dare sparked my ill-conceived dissertation, *From Folklore to Racecraft: The Myth of White Purity in Southern Tales*. Oh, who did I think I was? I was going to explain Southern folklore as shaping the history of the South, the history of white supremacy. What a fool! And still I spent years trying to turn it into a book that would secure tenure. As one of my mentors wrote in my termination letter, "It will take a lot more real literature and a lot fewer corncobby chronicles to bring this misguided manuscript into contemporary literary debates."

It started with a story I loved as a child. That was the betrayal; I had loved the story before I knew the message it held. In spring of first grade, we were supposed to take a field trip to see a production of *The Lost Colony* at Manteo. The trip was canceled, and instead we watched a low-budget educational film about Virginia Dare. It was right here, here! Ms. Beasly said, off the Carolina coast. We recited like sheep: On August 18, 1587, Virginia, the daughter of Ananias Dare and Eleanor White Dare was born, the "first English baby in the new world."

When Virginia was a week old, her grandfather, colony governor John White, sailed back to England for supplies. Because of the war with Spain, he wasn't able to return for three years. When he finally made it back to Roanoke Island, Virginia Dare had vanished, along with the entire colony. How I loved that story! The original "gone girl."

In the school film, an expressive reenactor played John White, scanning the shoreline hand to forehead, his buckled shoe on the ship's bow. We could hear the soft scraping as the flyboat approached the reedy shore, and the shuffle of his fancy shoes through the leaves as he approached the abandoned camp. His face was full of soap opera shock as he searched among the trees until he found the word CROATOAN etched in a tree trunk, the only trace of the colony.

Then the movie ended and the story got good. Had Virginia Dare really disappeared? Ms. Beasly asked the class. *Noooo* came the reply. She became a beautiful young woman who was loved by many men, befriended by Manteo, chief of the Croatoan, and desired by a rival chief, Okisko.

A mean old witch doctor, according to Ms. Beasly, turned Virginia into a white doe when she rejected him. The "evil" Indian Wanchese, an enemy of the English, also desired Virginia, but she spurned him. When she became a deer, he schemed to kill her with a silver arrow.

Meanwhile, Okisko learned he could turn the doe into the lovely Virginia again with the arrow of an oyster shell. When he saw the white doe drinking from a spring in the forest where the lost colony had been, he aimed and released his pearly arrow. At the same moment, Wanchese released his silver arrow and the doe's heart was doubly pierced. The white doe resumed her form as Virginia Dare, but she was dying.

Again, I cried. Again, Ms. Beasly told me it was okay, that it was a story with a sad end, but it was important to know our history and our heritage.

Why was Wanchese evil? I wanted to know.

He was an Indian who hated the English.

But why? Maybe Virginia was in love with Okisko, and she ran off with him, and he taught her to—

"So many questions and notions," Ms. Beasly said, with what I came to know as the deadly Southern serial smile. "Let's have snack."

"But why do all the ladies die in our stories, Ms. Beasly?"

"Snack time!"

"But Ms. Beasly, why was Wanchese evil? Maybe he wasn't."

"Don't talk ugly, Rachel."

"But—"

"Gather around, class. Who wants to serve the Kool-Aid?"

FIVE

ON THE FIRST two attempts, I pull into the driveway, back out and drive off. Days later, I try again. I leave the car and cross the yard and still don't know what I might do. She stands at the half open storm door.

"Rachel."

She holds a baby, who is looking away, into the house, her little leg a handle across her mother's stomach. It is the leg of my niece, wrapped around the hip of Garland's partner.

"Hi, Jewel."

I'm struck, as always, by her beauty, and by her expression, which shifts between open and guarded too quickly to track. The baby kicks her chubby little foot and rests it on the doorframe. She turns and smiles, rubbing her head against Jewel's chest.

"Hello, Lyric."

Jewel looks at her daughter. Maybe, like me, she is searching for Garland in the baby's face. Lyric watches her mother closely, leaning back so that her light blue T-shirt rides up, revealing her tiny belly button.

"Everybody hates her name. They say it's too 'woo-woo,' like Moonbeam or something."

Lyric laughs and leans back farther, raising her arms to the sky.

"It's perfect, Jewel. She's beautiful."

"Well, that won't help."

There is so much sadness in her voice that Lyric and I look at her, one of us without words, and one of us without the right ones.

She blinks down at the baby, then squints at her and kisses the child's head. Lyric puts her fist in her mouth and begins to gnaw, absorbed and serious.

"Would you like to come in?"

I'm desperate to talk about Garland, and she probably senses my desperation. But I have to be calm, not scare her the way I scare myself.

"I came to invite you to dinner. I'm sorry it's taken so long."

I stand with one foot on the threshold, hesitant to cross, and Jewel doesn't try again.

"We were supposed to have dinner with your parents before they died. Your mom called me the week before the wreck. I hadn't told them about Lyric. I wasn't ready. But word got around."

"I hoped they would contact you. They were just so broken up about Garland. They felt rejected."

"Yeah. They weren't thrilled about the two of us either."

"You were younger than Garland, and you weren't married."

"I'm also Black."

"I'm sorry for the way—I know it wasn't easy for you, Jewel."

"Nothing is easy for anybody around here. It's just that people like to believe they're better than they are."

"A writer I like says people are almost always better than their neighbors suppose."

"Depends on the neighbor, I guess. I take it this writer is not from a small Southern town." She smiles.

"True."

"What do you want, Rachel?"

"To meet Lyric, to see you both."

Lyric grasps Jewel's shirt and looks around sleepily. She has Jewel's heart-shaped face and Garland's light green eyes.

"You've been away a long time. You can't just breeze in and out of people's lives."

"Come to dinner Saturday. Please?"

She nods her head and looks at me with kindness and apprehension. "We'll come."

"Do you have any dietary restrictions?"

She laughs. "Dietary restrictions! You have been gone a long time. I eat everything."

"Say six? Is that too late for Lyric?" The eagerness in my voice making us both uncomfortable.

"Six. We'll be there," she says, as though to warn, *back off.* "We know our way."

ON THE DRIVE HOME, I scan the road for animals, white does or dream dogs, and think of all the crippling losses in these Southern woods, and about sacrifice, but that was my parents' domain, something I was excluded from, possibly protected from, like hearing the voice of the Lord. I lost my faith ages ago, to my parents' sorrow. Garland was their greater grief. He had separated from them, and from the farm. He had moved in with Jewel. My parents could never admit that any of this bothered them, that Garland didn't want their land, and that he had slowly excluded them from his life.

I had dutifully visited them twice a year, but this had only reinforced Garland's absence. Recently, I had encouraged my parents to meet him halfway, and to get to know Jewel.

"Leave it lay," Dad said. "You never could."

We were driving home after a failed attempt to give away Garland's shoes. We had gathered up the ones he'd left behind, and Dad put them in a garbage bag, along with Garland's collection of baseball caps. We headed to the dump, where Duck managed things and sold metal for scrap. They say he has picked every president since Eisenhower. Dad asked Duck if he could use some caps.

"No!" Duck shouted. "No cats!"

"Caps, not cats," Dad said. They had a good laugh, and Duck said he had no use for either. So we took the bag of empty shoes back home and returned them to gather dust in the closet, which was sadder than seeing them on a stranger's feet.

At the curve before Spivey's, Dad stopped the truck. He got out and stood in the road, looking over the field and trees. He turned his face toward the sky, but still he didn't speak. I got out, too, and climbed in the back of the truck where I used to sit when I was a child, on the hump above the wheel. I didn't fit comfortably anymore, so I moved up onto the railing. He walked back to the truck and put his hand on the door handle, bowed his head and didn't move. I thought of how once during high school I had punished him by not speaking to him for three and a half weeks and he had failed to notice. This was after I found out he had warned Tobias away from me. I didn't know what he said, only that it worked. I wanted to ask him why he had done it, but we had never been able to speak freely. It was Mom who broke the silence, sitting us down at the table and saying, You two have to talk. We sat across from each other, with our stubborn scowls, until Dad said, Pass the pie. And we ate in silence, angrily shoveling the cream cheese and canned cherries into our mouths.

He walked around the truck and lowered the tailgate, slow and careful. Then he stretched out his hand, and I took it and jumped down. When has he ever taken my hand? I wondered, even as he dropped it and began walking. I followed, thinking with each footstep, maybe I could ask him now. Garland's death was the only significant event we had ever truly shared, and in a terrible way, it could be our one chance to connect. I stared at his back, willing myself to say something. My father always walked ahead, he never turned. I could ask him now, I thought, groping for an opening phrase. I couldn't. A few days later we parted with a promise:

"I'll be back soon." But I wasn't.

"We'll be here." And they weren't.

PASSING THE CHURCH on my way home from Jewel's, I see a scene unfolding in the gravel parking lot. Three boys are shoving a smaller boy, who backs against an overturned bike. Tom. I pull over, and the boys scatter like birds, watching and waiting until the last second. They take off running, and by the time I get out of the car they are across the lot and on their way.

I know who you are! I almost call. Something in their gait, their backward glance; I bet I could tag most of them with a family name.

Tom looks at me from behind his bike. I must seem a hundred years old. May as well be shaking a cane and raising a fist at the fleeing bullies.

"Are you all right?"

He nods, looking down at his bleeding knee, which is so naked, such an innocent schoolboy knee, that I'm overcome for this young misfit.

"Tom?"

He glances up from his crouch, feeling the bike frame as for broken bones.

"Can I take you home?"

He doesn't answer, but shrugs and shuffles his feet in the gravel. A pony-tailed child skips toward us across the grassy churchyard.

"Tom! Tom! Give me a ride on the handlebars." She stops in front of us. "Why are you bleeding? Did you crash?"

"You live by yourself on that farm?" Tom asks, ignoring the girl.

"All alone, except for Junebug. Who's this?"

"I'm Lily Rae. I'm five."

"My little sister."

"You live on a farm?" Lily says. "Do you have horses?"

"No, no horses."

"Don't you want horses? A farm needs horses."

"It's not a horse farm."

"Not even one?"

"Not so far."

"We have horses, don't we Tom? We wash them in the bathtub and feed them apples from the crabapple tree."

"They're not real."

"Are too! Mine is a white horse named Priscilla Lorraine. Tom's is brown but he calls her Red."

"They're pretend," Tom says. "And Red is red like a red-bone hound dog."

"He's really more brown," Lily says.

"How do you know?"

"I can see him, Tom! I can see Red!"

"Can I give you two equestrians a ride home?"

Tom walks his bike to the car, and I put it in the trunk. They squabble over the front seat before Tom opens the door and slides in. Lily's fine brown hair is falling out of her ponytail and she pouts her juice-stained lips as I open the back door.

She quickly recovers her good spirits and buckles her seatbelt.

"Click it or ticket!"

When I start the car, she begins to talk, with a natural curiosity and a deadpan delivery.

"Do you believe in God?"

"Do you?"

"Yes, silly. Everybody believes in God."

It is not my place to expand the mind of this five-year-old and I'm glad the drive is a short one.

Tom rolls his eyes. "She asks everybody, now that grandma has moved in with us and takes her to Sunday school."

"Do you believe in heaven?"

Throughout my life, I have relied heavily on the repeat-the-question technique, which works well, as people often want a chance to answer the very thing they've asked.

"Do you believe in heaven, Lily?"

"Yes! Grandpa is there."

"That's good. Who else?"

"Mr. Bob's horse, Lady. She died and went to heaven so now grandpa has a horse to ride through the streets paved with gold."

"You really like horses."

Tom presses his foot against the edge of the mat that has curled up from the car floor. Methodically, he goes back and forth, over and over it, like picking a scab.

"I wish I was a horse," Lily says, "a beautiful horse with long hair in ribbons. What about you, Tom? Don't you want to be a horse?"

"I'd rather be a deer. They get to run free in the woods."

He continues to rub the mat, like an animal that will gnaw off its foot to escape the trap.

"What were you doing back there, in the parking lot?"

"Nothing."

"I thought I saw a hole near your bike."

"I like to look for sharks' teeth in the rocks."

"I used to do that. What about the hole?"

"Those boys told me I should dig to China."

"I did that, too."

"Did you ever get there?"

"No."

"Is China as far as heaven?" Lily asks. "What if China is

invisible, like our horses and heaven? Then how do you know it's real?"

"I know China exists. It's a country."

"Have you ever been there?"

"No."

"Then how do you *know* know?"

"I'll show you on a map."

"I hope heaven is a real place," Lily says. "Can you show us on the map? Do you really think there are horses there?"

"I'm sure heaven has whatever you think it has."

Their grandmother comes to meet us when I pull up. She is solid footed and silver haired, but not very old for a grandmother. "What's wrong?" she asks anxiously. "What happened?"

Tom jogs up the steps, skirting his grandmother and slamming the door behind him. Lily is slower, singing about a sparkling pony and twirling her hair as I get Tom's bike from the trunk and lean it against a blue hydrangea bush.

"Some boys were bullying Tom in the church parking lot. He scraped his knee."

Lily hugs the woman's legs as we introduce ourselves. Her name is Irma. She moved in to help keep the children after her husband died in an accident at the spinning mill, which is closing at the end of the year.

"Tom is being held back a year in school. He has dyslexia, though he's smart as all get-out. But these neighborhood boys, they just taunt and vex him no end."

"He's a bright kid."

"Do you think so?" she asks, coming closer. "We're looking for a tutor. Didn't I hear someone say you were a teacher?"

"I taught at a college, but Tom needs a specialist. They should be able to help you at the school."

"They say they don't have the funds or the staff to spare. Tom has to take the bus over an hour each way. And those same boys ride the bus with him. His father, Burl, says he needs to spend less time worrying about those boys and more time learning to be a man." She averts her eyes. "That's why he insisted on giving him the shotgun now. It was my husband's. Burl wants Tom in the woods, hunting and doing who knows what, manly things I suppose."

Tom comes out and stands beside Lily. I want to tell her not to listen, not to be vetoed, to take the gun away right now, but a woman has little say here, and even less in another man's house.

SIX

JUNE SNOOZES, AND I try to work, on a baggy, shapeless article about metamorphosis as exile and escape, but also as death. In my last year in New York, I had been spending days in museums instead of writing. At the Met Cloisters, which had been assembled using some of the stones of European abbeys, I had become obsessed with a fifteenth-century tapestry that shows Actaeon happening upon the goddess Diana bathing in the forest. A startled Diana splashes him with water and changes him into a deer to be devoured by his own hounds. The tapestry beautifully captures Actaeon metamorphosing into a stag. Antlers sprout from his hard blond head, and the hunting hounds immediately see that he is meat. Actaeon the stag is killed and eaten by his own beloved dogs, who do not recognize their master, as his unknowing hunting friends watch, wishing Actaeon was there to see.

"What do you call an academic with too many interests?" the sociologist, Lucas, asked one night during what I thought was our playful phase. "Multipotentialities," I teased. "Untenured," he said.

I have set up my desk in the kitchen, at the long knotty pine table, but I can't stop looking out the window at the fall fields and bordering trees. Reading my academic writing, I barely recognize the words. It's like looking at a specimen under a bell jar, isolated, preserved without context, static, dead. Outside, the only sound is that of the shrill-voiced cicadas, who sing without cease. The harvest is almost over. Then it will be a long winter of fallow fields and country quietude, and I will have to make a decision.

I flip through the strange notes I've written over the last week, my revisionist renderings of the Witch Bride and Shiloh Light. Another project that's clearly going nowhere. My old notebooks are full of the Virginia Dare draft that never saw publication. The unfinished chapter on V. Dare, white purity, and purity ring ceremonies makes my face burn with shame. I told a personal story of the purity ring to a Columbia professor I admired . . . no, respected . . . no, *loved*. I wanted to *be* her. I wanted to live in her organized way, in her snug little city office with its red worn rug and the kettle in the corner surrounded by little packages of tea that she offered freely and generously to anyone who came to her office. She even remembered that I loved Constant Comment, with its silly name and delightful scent of cinnamon and orange. I was taking her evening writing class as a way to think through my troubled relationship to storytelling. This instructor was not as famous as she would later become, when she would stop answering my emails. Unlike many professors, she was generous with office hours, and I made myself go. She was interested in my background, and remarked on my crooked canine, my accent, and said that my almost belligerent stare reminded her of Carson McCullers in those Bettmann photos.

I wanted to please this professor; I wanted to bring her something McCullers-level memorable, so I told her about my purity ceremony and how I didn't know how to write about it. She stirred my tea and said how awful you were taught that, that your only value lies between your legs. Well, I said, and smiled—as always wanting to please her, bringing her my childhood like a toy offering to a cat—the lesson didn't take. That's good, she said, and looked at me with pity and possibly a tinge of repulsion. I felt the double shame that I sometimes do, of being stranded, the shame I felt for who I was and where I was from, and the second deeper shame, hard to put into words, the shame of knowing I would perform my life if it was the only entry into this world, her world that I wanted to belong to. Knowing, too, that I would always be stranded. That I would always be a double, dissolvable, not solid: I don't believe in God. *But I could.*

What I told her wasn't true. I never had a purity ceremony and my father never placed a ring on my finger. I was willing to spin a lie to this professor, a complete fabrication of a supposedly true story that I wanted her to help me turn into a novel. The duplicity! The deception. I wasn't able to tell her the real story, the traumatic event that shaped my youth and was too perfectly a Southern cliché to give to the world. As though to say, yes, it's true, the rural South is the terrifying place you believe it to be, where unspeakable things happen to children who go on to pretend it never happened because to tell would be to reinforce the awful stereotype of place with the truth that proves that rule.

JUNE INSISTS ON A WALK, so we set off, passing fields and farms and not seeing a soul. Behind the field across the dirt road, a tract of young pine stands in dark indifference. Farther back is an older copse of trees that butts against timberland. Warrens has offered to buy the entirety for pulpwood. I have to figure out what to do with a farm that was meant for my brother. If I sell it, I can, for the first time in my life, do anything I want, until the money runs out. But the slit of an *I* between "anything" and "want" is just wide enough to fall through.

The tracts of land are named for the families that own them, but the flimsiness of ownership is more apparent now, as tobacco farmers scramble to find the new moneymaker, hydroponic tomatoes or hemp or manure-eating red worms. I'm considering possible tobacco replacements for my inherited land, but what do I know about farming?

Three figures come toward us in single file, the Gurkin sisters. They pass in silence, each responding to my greeting with a curt nod. Vasta, the oldest, leads. She must be seventy by now, and she strides ahead unsmiling and free of fear. The middle one, whose name I can't remember, follows close behind, offering a hesitant smile and hurrying to keep up. The youngest lags along, singing under her breath. Crazy Annie they call her. The sisters never married, and have lived in the same farmhouse all their lives. Their reticence and refusal to marry has aroused suspicion. I suddenly recall the rumor that Vasta and her sisters might have had something to do with their father's death. They are referred to meanly as the three little pigs, because of the way they walk one behind the other down the empty road, instead of three abreast.

House of straw, house of sticks, house of bricks. If only it were so easy in life to know what endures.

ENTERING THE HOUSE, I hear, or think I hear, the noise upstairs. Time to open the attic door. The heat oppresses as I trudge up the steps, and a deep judge voice says, *All rise. All rise, with the heat.* I'm waiting for the sentence that never came. The dormer windows face south and the attic is always hot, always stuffy, always closed—the family evidence room. I scan the floor and walls, seeking the noisy culprit. Nothing. My arms tingle wrist to elbow, the hairs like wind-ruffled wheat. It's because of Garland's corner. His baseball bat leans against the wall, and his glove and cleats sit shockingly empty on the floor. The things he left behind; the things my parents couldn't part with.

A single snapshot is on top of Garland's box, as though someone has left it lying out in the open. I must be about three in the picture, scrambling off our parents' bed as Garland reaches out, his arm frozen in eternal protection. A gun rack with two rifles is mounted on the wall above our heads. This was before my father kept the guns locked in the pump house, the key in his pocket. Who had taken this snapshot? And why were we in our parents' room where we weren't allowed to play? Some ghost took it and placed it here, a spectral biography: Garland, guns, and me, framed and locked in the silent shot. I gather the photo, the baseball bat, and inexplicably, a blender. I'm sweating and queasy; the taste of salt is on my lips.

I feel faint and lie down on the attic floor. I used to come up here at night when I couldn't sleep to think of everyone below me, put away safely like bread in the breadbox, while I floated above. I wore a long lavender nightgown and copper bracelets. When the hunters killed deer, they had to tag the dead. The tag dangled from a copper wire they ran through the deer's soft, unfeeling ear. Dad and Garland saved the wires for me to make bracelets, and many nights I would take them from my jewelry box, which opened to a tiny twirling ballerina playing "Swan Lake." I would lie on the attic floor, take a breath, bite a bracelet, and try to slip my skin like the witch in the story.

Skin, skin, you know me?

I bit the bracelets until my mouth bled. If I could fly away, maybe I could find Professor.

Skin, skin, you know me?

I am on my back, bolted to the attic floor. I'm older now; it's harder, but I close my eyes and feel some part of myself lifting up and away from my body.

Skin, skin, this is me.

A pressure in my heart, a pain. I sit up, gasping, my soul panting, possibly, impossibly transforming from a woman to a witch, a werewitch. It's voluntary, like the werewolf in Virgil, who hides away in the woods with poisonous herbs and arouses souls from the depths of their tombs. But I want those tombs to stay closed.

TOBIAS SHOWS UP with tomatoes and moonshine. I thank him, and he asks for a glass.

"You don't waste any time."

"I knew you wouldn't make the first move," he says.

"Is this a move?"

"It's my best moonshine, tastes like firewater. Have a sip."

"No thanks."

"Well sit outside with me while I drink it. You need a spotter to drink 'shine. And I want to show you something."

We settle on the porch swing, though I keep to one side, and June thrusts her nose between us, but, I note, closer to Tobias.

"See the lightning bugs?" he asks, looking toward the garden, where the magical beetles are beginning to glow. "Bet you don't have those in New York."

"We do, in Central Park. They're fireflies." There are words I choose depending on where I am. That's one of the reasons I am a fake and fractured self. Once, at an academic dinner party, my advisor asked me to feed her dog supper. We call it supper in the South, too, I had said, stupidly, delightedly. The dogs have supper, she said, without a trace of malice. *We* have dinner.

"I was thinking today about the time we went to Atlantic Beach together. Do you remember, Rachel?"

"It was the first time I saw the ocean."

"I didn't think you'd go when I asked you."

"It was the beach. You had a car."

"Wow, romantic."

"I wanted to see it."

"Remember, we got caught in a summer storm."

"And took shelter under the pier. We were soaked."

"Then we ate shrimp burgers and hush puppies at the pier restaurant."

"On the way home we stopped at the Kicking Machine near New Bern."

"You could give yourself a kick in the pants. I haven't thought of that in ages. Bet it's not there anymore."

"There were several old shoes bolted on a wheel, right? You just bent over and turned the hand crank."

"What I remember is how hard you kicked yourself," he says.

"Left a bruise."

"I know."

I will myself not to flush, and fail. In high school, the psychology teacher, who was also the PE teacher, liked to say to the class, "I bet we can't make Rachel Ruskin blush." And my face would go wine red while everyone laughed and laughed.

"I was nervous calling your dad to tell him we were going to wait out the storm."

After we kicked ourselves at the Kicking Machine, we huddled under the awning, and ended up in a redbrick motel with green walls and sandy sheets.

"He trusted you."

"He shouldn't have."

He clenches his jaw, and the delicate spot under his cheekbones hollows then fills, in a way I remember without realizing I remembered. When we ended, which was inevitable, I told myself it was just a flirtation from my youth, one easy to forget.

"So how do you find it," he asks, "home?"

Home is another word I had stricken from my vocabulary, a four-letter word, same as *love* and *hate*.

"I was thinking of the time after the beach when you stood me up," I say, changing the subject. "You avoided me."

"Your dad gave me a talking to. He said you were set on going to college."

"The paternalism!" I blurt, and it's almost a relief to feel the old anger at my father that I haven't felt since his death. In an odd way, it makes me closer to him. "You wouldn't have held me back, Tobias." And neither would you, old man, I say silently to my father.

He laughs. "I know. But why complicate things and anger your parents? It seemed like you'd all been through enough."

"What does that mean?"

"After the accident with Rufus," he says, and stops.

We watch the fireflies flash and I feel the heat on my face, as though I, too, am signaling in the dimming light.

Tobias asks what I'm thinking about, and I say the ocean.

"The time we went together?"

"No, I was thinking how my family, the four of us, never went. It's only an hour and a half away, but I didn't see the ocean until I went with you."

I imagine us, my parents, Garland, and me standing in the Atlantic Beach parking lot, peeking around the car to see the ocean while eating sandwiches from the trunk with seagulls keening and swooping around us. We would have to eat at the car so we wouldn't get sand in the sandwiches, my mother would say, but it was just what we would do because my parents were of the place and generation when people without means clung to a shabby formality. You packed your lunch and you ate it, neatly, privately. I moved to New York on Amtrak with a duffel bag and two pimento cheese sandwiches wrapped in foil. My family never did go to the ocean together. The only sand I saw between my parents' toes was from the field, and that was a darker dirt that didn't wash off with water alone.

"Your dad is the only small farmer I know of who kept growing tobacco after the buyout. It doesn't make sense."

"Why do you think he did that after they took away the subsidy? There's no price control anymore. It's risky for small farmers, not to mention that the plant itself is poison."

"He was stubborn. He'd always grown it so he was going to keep growing it."

"Corn feeds; tobacco pays. Isn't that North Carolina's motto?"

"Not anymore."

This farm won't make anyone rich, but if Tobias adds the entirety of Four Corners, he will dominate this little county where fields have been corned and soybeaned to death.

"I haven't decided what to do, Tobias."

"No rush."

He's happy to pick up where we left off when I was eighteen. But I send him away with his memories and moonshine, while I sit in the dark wondering what I will do with the time that doesn't happen here.

SEVEN

ON SATURDAY, I head to Greenvale with my grocery list. Greenvale is what people here call town. Shiloh is unincorporated, a village, a hamlet really, and Greenvale is a town of nine-thousand-odd souls, and the closest place that qualifies as incorporated. In between, the areas are known by their markers and makers: crossroads (Douglas and Spivey), churches (Beaver Dam and Old Ford), ponds (Woodard and Bonner).

Grabbing the rental car keys from their hook on the washboard I see my mom's lonely leather keychain. Why had I bought that silly fob and foisted it on my mother, who used it till the end of her life because she, like my father, couldn't bear waste? For years, they would use things they never would have chosen simply because they were there. For a decade my father had been wearing Uncle John's tasseled loafers and red ties because they were given to him after the funeral. He had walked miles in a dead man's shoes.

They totaled their car in the wreck. It was a clean total, dad, mom, Buick, all dead, after an exhausted long-haul trucker hit them head on. I consider my rental car—economy, unlimited miles—just behind my dad's Ford pickup, wolf ferrier, work truck.

In the perfectly impersonal rental, AC blasting, and the radio off because all stations are fuzzy, I back out of the drive listening to the satisfying sound of tires crunching gravel. After twenty years of noisy commuter trains, I have finally found the quiet car.

THE GROCERY STORE takes time. I haven't cooked for anyone in a long while, and never for my niece and sister-in-law. In New York I picked up a few things here and there, now I'm a stranger in a strange land pushing a cart through the frigid airplane hangar of cans and bottles and boxes. I buy pasta and fresh basil and the ingredients for marinara sauce. I pause at the pineapple-hummingbird cake, a regional delicacy. On impulse, I add the ingredients to my cart: banana, pineapple, eggs, pecans, cream cheese, butter, and powdered sugar. I leave off the cinnamon, nutmeg, and vanilla extract, confident my mother wouldn't be caught dead with those items missing from the pantry. But she *has* been caught dead, and on the drive home, this becomes important, whether the nutmeg will in fact be on the shelf, in the cramped closet with its old wood boards and stained green-and-white sticky lining. I was going to help her replace it last year over the Christmas holiday. But my tenure case was pending, and in the end, I had come only for a couple of days. Maybe my parents had tried to understand my stress, even though it didn't seem so. They found the notion of tenure slightly ridiculous. To them, I was a teacher. Surely someone with a PhD (seven years!) would always find work in cities where such things made sense. The things that made sense here were cents per pound and sins of neighbors and scents of animal manure and blights brought on the wind, which might shift at any moment.

MY ARMS ARE full as I enter the house, banging the door shut. Sorry Mom. Unpacking groceries in the kitchen, I turn to see my parents as they were only a year ago, on one of my last visits. I had acquiesced to go to church with them that morning, and after, we entered the house in the midday heat.

"Why don't you take Garland's room?" Mom asked. Immediately, the old tension was tapped in my father, in me. "It's cooler," she added.

The three of us were awkward once Garland's name had been spoken. Mom began heating oil in the old cast iron skillet and dredging flounder in cornmeal.

Dad was carrying the family Bible that went to church with them twice a week, and he took his place at the head of the table, standing behind his chair as he looked down at the pages. The sermon had been on Abraham and Isaac. *Take now thy son, thine only son . . .*

"Your eyes getting worse, Dad?"

"No, my arm's just getting too short."

Mom looked over from the stove. "Remember how you used to love reciting from the Old Testament, Rachel? Do you still read it?"

"No."

She frowned and lifted a fish with a pair of tongs, placing it on a paper-towel-covered platter. "Ecclesiastes. That was your favorite. Remember?"

"That was a long time ago, Mom."

"Not really," Dad said. "Not in the scheme of things."

When we sat down to eat, Mom asked me to say the blessing.

"I returned and saw under the sun, that the race is not to the swift, nor the battle to the strong, neither yet bread to the wise, nor yet riches to men of understanding, nor yet favor to men of skill, but time and chance happen to them all. Amen."

"You do remember," she said.

"Happen*eth*," Dad said.

THAT AFTERNOON, my father was in the garden digging sweet potatoes. My mother wanted me to join him. She was always trying to make things better between us. The truth was we had little to say.

I picked up a spading fork awkwardly.

"It's late," he said. "I should have dug them sooner, before the rain."

We worked in silence for a while, tossing potatoes into the plastic bucket with a satisfying plunk. I regretted the silence that encased us like an invisible carapace, and I looked around, searching for a topic of conversation.

"What happened to the field at Birdie's Place? That's usually your best tobacco plot, but I see there's nothing planted there this year."

He stopped digging and looked west, toward his favorite field, and then back at me. "You didn't know? Granville Wilt took it. We had to destroy the whole crop. It wounded every plant to the root. It's a terrible disease."

"How do you recognize it?" I asked, knowing what he'd say but needing to hear, like begging for a bedtime story I knew by heart. I remembered Granville Wilt from my childhood, because of the fear it struck in farmers' hearts, and the way they talked about it, with an almost reverential reprehension.

"It doesn't matter if you recognize it or not, if it's here, it's here. When you can see it, it's already too late. It got to the patch near the drying house, and then it rained, and spread."

The soil had that yellow cast it gets after a big rain, like things were turned upside down, and the light was coming up from the ground, the sky still dark and wet.

"The wilt is such a blight when it's in the soil."

"What gets in the soil?"

"Bacteria. It's the bacteria that gets in the soil and turns the plant yellow, wilts it down in a day or two. When the tobacco is almost mature—the plant can be pretty today and tomorrow it's wilted and in two or three days it's hanging from the stalk like a wet rag. There's not a thing to be done. If it rains, the water spreads it around, wilts the field in sections. Once the wilt takes the crop there's nothing you can do. It's a matter of days, that's how fast it is. And you can't plant there for five years, seven to be certain. You can't plant in soil that has the blight."

We continued digging. I wasn't handy with a garden tool, and I gouged a couple of potatoes loosening them from the soil. He didn't say anything, but I saw that he saw. I put the fork aside and plunged my hands directly into the earth, carefully taking the Carolina Rubies from the ground.

"So there's no cure?"

"The only cure is time. You can't plant in blighted soil," he said again, and sunk his shovel neatly in the dirt. "But if you're patient, you can try again, when the soil has regenerated."

I considered bacteria and blight and my slight surprise at his using the word *regenerated*. I wondered whether our own family could be regrown or restored. It seemed unlikely, but it would be the most significant way we could honor Garland. "Dad, why did we lie about what happened the night Professor died?"

"What should we have done?"

"Told the truth."

He looked at me then, with what seemed like bewilderment, but his expressions had always been hard to read. "You were a child."

"So was Garland."

"He was the boy, Rachel. You were his younger sister."

Just a girl, it was true. I had always thought the message was in the soil here, that boys were more valued; they owned the land, reaped the rewards, and when something went wrong, whether accident or insult, the burden was theirs. But it was through the church the message was made clear: A woman's body is her house, the minister used to say, when preaching wifely submission and the cult of domesticity. I had wanted to shout, And what is a man's body? An empty old barn?

"Are you proposing something, Rachel, or just talking?"

I had not been proposing, but I wasn't going to ignore his tone, which held both challenge and opportunity. "We could tell the truth now."

"What good would that do?"

"The guilt ruined us, Dad. We never recovered—not any of us."

He walked away and emptied the bucket of potatoes into the wheelbarrow, then returned with the bucket and started digging again, farther from me.

"You know why," he said suddenly. "You know why I still grow tobacco?"

"No," I said, thinking, *because you're a stubborn stubborn man*. "It's risky without the subsidies."

"Maybe so," he said. "You know that farm on Thirty-two, the one by the Raritan Lodge?"

"The one owned by Mennonites?"

He nodded. "They don't grow tobacco because they don't think it's right. They consider farming sacred work."

"Do you?" I waited, and he looked down the row and winced, the way he did when he didn't want to continue but felt called on to say something more.

"I grew tobacco. I grow tobacco. I have never taken much counsel."

I smiled then, and didn't say, That's the truth.

"You never have either," he added. I nodded; that was also true. "Our ancestors grew tobacco, and it came down to us that way, with all the rest. History," he said.

"Are you saying guns and tobacco and lies are just things as plain and solid as trees, and we should never consider any sort of change but we should just keep going in a straight line until we die?"

"Maybe I should have done something different, but this is what I did. I chose to stay. You chose to leave. This is what I can do."

You don't know what it was like for me, I wanted to say, but I knew it sounded childish, and might lead to begging for the sort of love he wasn't able to give. There was also the belief I'd had since that terrible night, that he wanted to hate me— though he couldn't, not quite—because he had had to sacrifice his son to protect me.

"It's this place," I said instead, and my voice was strained, almost a whisper. It's a mutilated ghost land, I almost added, but instead repeated, "It's this place."

"It's the world, Rachel."

"*This* is not the world," I said angrily, flinging my arm out.

"It is mine. A man can't live everywhere."

"Okay, Dad. You win."

"Not trying to win. Just trying to live by the land, where time and chance happens to us all."

"And sometimes, Dad, shit happen*eth*."

"Yes," he agreed, and gave a half laugh, which is the only kind he ever gave. "But that's covered under the first two."

"Time and chance? That's all life is?"

"What else is there, Rachel?"

I TIDY UP for Jewel and Lyric, make a salad, scrub the kitchen floor. On the radio one of Fred Phelps's granddaughters is being interviewed about her break from her family's church in Topeka, Kansas. She's in her early twenties, and she left one day when her family was at a military funeral, protesting gays and "their filthy manner of life." Her mother sent her a text that said, "Are you having a nice day?" and the young woman threw her phone down on the bed and left. Her family excommunicated her, as did the church, and she has no contact with anyone she used to know. She says their church "nitpicks" a person to death after she's left, and labels her either a whore or a rebel.

The interviewer talks to another twenty-something who is still in the church. She cries and cries as she says how wonderful her life is. "It's like a fairy tale," she says. "But it's not, it's real life!" She is asked whether she would rejoice if her three-year-old daughter were to get ill and die. "Yes," she says. "None of us are born innocent. We all deserve death every day."

I SIT ON the porch all afternoon, pretending to read, and staring off into the woods. The night that Professor, Garland, and I snuck away from the house, we were children. We were innocent. We were undeserving of death. It would not have occurred to us that it was even possible. We had already done everything there was to do that summer into fall—caught fireflies, baptized Professor in the swimming hole, eaten a tobacco worm. There was nothing left to do but to go into the woods to see the ghost of Joe Brooks and help him find his head.

When Jewel and Lyric pull up, I meet them at the car, trying, and failing, to disguise my relief. I had worried they would cancel. Now I worry we'll be too formal with each other.

"Make yourself at home," I say, and flinch as I open the door. Jewel was never made to feel at home here. My parents tolerated her, but they held her apart. They held everyone apart really, except Garland. And when he moved off the farm they retreated into their stoic silence.

"It's nice," Jewel says, gazing around the kitchen, a long room painted soft yellow with windows along two sides and the pine table stretching six feet down the middle. There aren't too many doodads, not too much bric-a-brac. My parents liked things sturdy and well made, neither elegant nor fussy.

Lyric beams and lifts her arms straight out. In her white gown with red piping and her raised arms, she's like a tiny fetching pope. I lean toward her and she submits to a kiss.

Jewel sits at the table to breastfeed Lyric while I simmer pasta sauce at the stove. Lyric is happily sucking and then turning her head away smiling and dribbling milk, then back to the breast, then away again. Every time I turn to Jewel, Lyric unlatches and looks at me, and Jewel covers her bare breast with her hand. I want to tell her she doesn't have to cover herself, but I don't want to embarrass her, or myself, so I stare into the saucepan as we continue our awkward choreography.

"How long will you stay, Rachel?"

"I'm not sure. I'm sorry I'm only meeting Lyric now. I didn't know she—"

"Existed?"

"Yes."

"Garland didn't know either. It was unexpected. I'm thirty-five; I wanted to be sure. I mentioned the other day that your mom invited us to dinner before the collision. It was only a few days before."

"They never met Lyric."

I ought to apologize, but it's stupidly inadequate. In the week before her death, my mom had left two or three voicemails, which was rare. I was nursing my academic wounds, and hadn't called back. Maybe she had wanted to tell me that she had a granddaughter, and I had, have, a niece.

"I thought there'd be time," she says. "And I was so angry after Garland died."

"We all were."

"I want to feel closer to him here," she says, "but I don't."

I follow her gaze around the room, realizing that's probably why she came, in search of Garland, some remnant of him in this house of old relics. Just as I invited her so that I could search for Garland in his daughter, to see if his spirit glimmers in this radiant child.

"His room is down the hall, first on the left. A few of his things are still there. Take what you want."

She hands Lyric to me, and we look at each other, apprehensive and appraising. *None of us are born innocent.* How ridiculous. We are born innocent. Then life has its way with us. Lyric kicks me in the side and I grab her foot. We're friends playing a game. I carry her around the kitchen, murmuring in her ear, showing her the light catcher I made for my mom in fourth grade. She puts her head directly against my chest, forehead first, like someone in prayer, or someone about to bang her head against a wall.

"Can I have this?" Jewel asks, holding Garland's old seed store T-shirt, worn thin as onionskin.

I nod, and Lyric lifts her arms, to be returned to her mother.

"Why that one?" I ask, as she drapes the shirt over Lyric's head and breathes in the scent.

A smile pulls at her mouth and she hesitates, deciding whether to say something.

"We had a joke," she says, a little embarrassed but meeting my gaze. "He liked to keep his clothes in the cedar chest, he loved the cedar scent."

"He always did, even when we were kids. He used the chest instead of the dresser."

"One night early in our relationship, we were dancing—"

"Garland, dancing?"

"Yes, he wasn't bad really. He had loose hips and a soft shuffle. Anyway, I smelled his shirt and he must have seen the surprised look on my face because he asked me if he stank. And I said, without thinking, 'You smell like storage.'" She laughs, and shakes her head. "It became a line we used with each other, to lighten the mood when we were fighting or sometimes out of the blue to make each other laugh."

I smile, and probably look a little confused.

"What?" she asks. "You didn't know white people smell like storage?"

Her smile is genuine, and I smile back, as Lyric looks up at her mother in adoration and blesses us with her gummy smile. I feel an unfamiliar flutter in my chest, and am seized with a foreign, almost violent, affection for Lyric, who is playing hide-and-seek with Garland's shirt. Jewel pulls the shirt off Lyric's head and the baby gurgles with delight. Jewel briefly covers her head again, and I feel a brief, irrational terror that she is a ghost baby disappearing before my eyes.

"I want to know Lyric, even though Garland is gone," I blurt, as Jewel shifts Lyric on her hip.

"You've been away a long time, Rachel. Let's take it slow."

Lyric pops her head up from Jewel's shoulder and grins toothlessly at us. Through the kitchen curtains pale presunset light sprays the sky. That pink reminds me of the postcard Lucas sent from London's National Gallery. I later found out the flowers the cherubic child is holding, pinks, are a symbol of marriage. The painting shows the Virgin Mary as not only the Mother, but also the Bride of Christ. I was with this man when Garland was dying alone in the woods.

"Are you afraid out here by yourself?" Jewel asks, while I toss the salad and put the pasta on.

"Why do you ask?"

"It's always seemed creepy to me."

There it is, in black and white. As women, we're both vulnerable, but for Jewel, there are added dangers.

"It's true I've always felt safer in New York. Strength in numbers; strength in strangers."

"It's always been a violent place," she says. "Still is. I live beside Mike Jackson's mom. Remember him? He went to prison for rape and murder."

"He was in my homeroom; we were only in tenth grade when that happened. And there was Eugene Emory."

"What was that for?"

"Drugs. He killed Lloyd Hodges."

"And Earl Wilson. He killed that man in a fight on a deer hunt."

"It's a significant percentage."

Jewel sways a milk-drunk Lyric in her arms, and June watches sleepily from her cushion in the corner.

"I'm surprised you'd come back after so many years."

"I considered this home once."

"You escaped."

"I failed."

"What do you mean?"

"I spent half my life studying other writers, other stories. I read and researched and taught for years. But I was up for tenure this year, that's when the university you work for—"

"I know what tenure means."

"Sorry. I—my parents didn't really understand."

"You'll have to break that habit, of explaining everything to people here."

Outside, streaks of orange hover over the hard, flat landscape. I don't know what to say.

"Anyway, I didn't get tenure."

"So here you are. Can't you teach somewhere else?"

"Maybe somewhere, but I'm off the tenure track. Damaged goods."

I don't think I've ever uttered that tainted term, a regional reference to unmarried pregnant women, violated virgins. In a place that believes in purity rings, a woman's virginity is still her worth.

"You're at a crossroads," Jewel says. "I don't think I could ever come back if I moved away. You either stay or go around here. There's no in-between."

"Do you ever think of leaving?"

"Sure. But it's harder now," she says, kissing Lyric's kicking foot.

Looking at the two of them in my parents' kitchen, I fall in love.

"Maybe there's something for me here."

"What could possibly be here for you? You live in New York."

"I live in books, really."

"Are you writing one yourself?" she asks, nodding to the pile at the end of the table, where my notebooks sit like slabs of sand, reinforcements against the flood of career disappointment that some nights threatens to swallow me whole.

"I don't know. Books have been my lifeline."

"Your life-lie?"

"Life*line*."

"I misheard you. My friend Tonya is involved with the Greenvale Rep. You knew they were renovating the old Turnage theater?"

"No," I say, dumping the bucatini in the boiling water.

"They are. Anyway, Tonya does scenery—she's a master carpenter—so I went to see their first production, Ibsen's *Wild Duck,* and I can't stop thinking about it. One of the characters says, 'If you take the life-lie away from an average person, you take away his happiness as well.'"

"Greenvale is producing Ibsen?"

"You sound like a snob, Rachel."

"Sorry. I didn't—What does 'life-lie' mean?"

"That we create these alternative lives for ourselves so we won't have to face the pain and disappointment of reality."

"We tell ourselves lies in order to live?"

"Often without realizing. Even if we do recognize our own life-lie, we can't necessarily change it. Acknowledging the lie might alter the course of your life, or destroy it."

Lyric watches gravely as I stir the pasta. Garland's daughter! She was once the size of a lentil, now she's a girl, with huge eyes and chubby knees. .

"Garland and I talked about moving to California," Jewel says abruptly, leaving me to wonder how much she knows about my family's life-lie. "No flat land, no humid heat, no family everywhere you step, no people telling you interracial parents are creating 'a nest of evil?'"

"That's awful. Someone said that?" I turn to her, the smooth wooden spoon in my hand.

"Annie Gurkin, Vasta's sister. It wasn't even malicious; it was more of a question. 'How could they call your beautiful family a nest of evil?' But everybody knows she's crazy." She laughs. "Other people thought it. We got looks. But honest Annie is the only one who repeated what she heard."

Annie, the third little pig. Annie, who was openly referred to as "damaged goods." I remembered her clearly because she had come up to me at the ballfield swingset when I was five or six. She was pregnant then, and I learned later the father of the child was assumed to be a member of her family. She was addled, people said, addled and damaged.

"Rachel, is something burning?"

The pasta foam swirls around the boiling water like yellow flotsam. The sauce bubbles and splatters and sticks to the burnt-bottomed pan. I throw it in the trash.

"Guess there's still no takeout?"

"Nope."

We eat grilled cheese sandwiches and hummingbird cake outside, and watch the sun refuse to go down.

"Jewel, how did you and Garland connect?" She is sitting on the top step, lightly rocking a sleeping Lyric. I stop the porch swing, where I've been softly keeping time with the two of them. "If you don't mind. It's really none of my business, but if you feel like talking about him at all."

She tenses and give a terse shake of the head.

"I hadn't seen him in ages. I was living in Greenvale—the bank made me manager after my MBA—and only came home to see the folks and Palmer, and then only straight to the house and straight back to Greenvale. There's not really anywhere to hang out around here. Not that I would want to."

Jewel looks out toward the fields, and turns back to me with an inscrutable expression.

"I was working nights at the Meeting Place restaurant to help out a friend, and Garland started coming in and sitting at my table. After that he began leaving things on the hood of my car at the bank—strawberries in June, blueberries in July, tomatoes in August. I finally told him he better ask me out before fall, because I wasn't wild about turnips."

"That sounds like him. I hadn't spoken to him in ages, but on 9/11, he sent me a text in New York. All it said was, 'Start walking south, and I'll pick you up in my truck.'"

"He was a man of few words, but they were always the ones you needed."

The first fireflies blink on. Soon it will be dark, and I realize I don't know where they disappear to, in the deeper dark.

"We should go. It's her bedtime."

I walk them to the car and they drive away, their red brake lights flashing briefly, leaving me with a sense of wonder and loneliness so piercing I want to chase after them. I begin to run down the drive, but they are gone.

EIGHT

ALL OF THE next morning, I think of Lyric's blissful face. I try to put her out of my mind and turn to the task of weeding the garden, but I find myself smiling again as her image floats before me. Babies can't help but smile, and we can't help but smile back, I reassure myself. None of us can escape biology.

Through the day the idea takes hold that I have to talk to Professor's parents if I am to be an aunt to Lyric. If not apology and absolution, then at least a bowing of my head, an acknowledgement. I failed with Roberta, so in the afternoon I go to Minister Swain.

The church is as it ever was, modest, white, the steeple pointy as a witch's hat. No clock, no bells. Like thousands of others all across the country. SHILOH CHURCH OF CHRIST, the white iron sign says, staked in a brick base spotted with pansies. I walk around to the back, and find the door to the reception hall unlocked. Inside, a light shines from the half-open office door, and I knock gently and peer inside.

"Minister Swain?"

He comes from behind his desk to greet me, moving stiff-hipped across the thin tan carpet. He hugs me, awkwardly, and I hug him back, also awkwardly, and we circle around in this clumsy embrace like two bears obeying a circus command.

"I hope you don't mind the interruption."

"Not at all. How are you Rachel?" he asks, and gestures for me to sit in the wooden chair across from his desk.

"Still numb, or getting to know the numbness better."

"That's to be expected. It was a shock, and a loss, for all of us. Your parents were pillars of the church and the community, as you know."

"Thank you. How is—" I start to say "your family," but quickly shift to "Roberta."

He smiles wanly. "She said you went to see her. She told you about this awful Pick's disease."

I nod and he leans across the desk, clasping his big hands. In my childhood I was fascinated by his huge hands. There were several objects around the church that I focused on to get through the interminable Sunday service, and Minister Swain's knobbly, knuckly hands were one of them.

"What about you, Rachel?"

"I have no immediate plans."

"Don't you have to get back to your life in the city, to teaching?"

"No. I'm at a lose end, a loose end, I mean." In an effort to change the subject, I ask about the sermon he's working on.

"It's the story of Hannah and Samuel. Do you know it?"

"Vaguely. She was barren and begged God for a child."

"Right. She's the second wife of Elkanah. His first wife has children, but Hannah does not."

I flinch at this reminder of parenthood, and don't know how to talk to this father about his dead son.

"Then God answers her, and she has Samuel, whom she has promised to give to the church. She weans him, then gives him up, and praises God with her Psalm: 'The Lord killeth, and maketh alive: he bringeth down to the grave, and bringeth up.'"

"It's a beautiful Psalm," I say, because even as a nonbeliever I can appreciate the language I learned in the King James version in this very church.

"Is there anything I can do for you, Rachel?"

"The part I remember is that she made him a coat," I say, thinking of Professor and the green jacket.

"She did. And she visited him for the annual sacrifice."

"It must have been very hard to give him up."

A shadow passes over his face. It is not a blush, but a darkening that seems to drop from his forehead like a curtain. "He bringeth low, and he lifteth up."

I can't avoid it any longer. "Minister Swain, I want to talk to you about that night in the woods with Professor, Rufus."

His face is anguished as he lifts his large hands to press his temples.

"Coming back has made the memory almost physical. And I have a niece now. I need to live more honestly."

"Rachel, I know what happened was an accident," he says, though I can see he is shaken. "If you are seeking forgiveness, for whatever reason, you must ask God."

I feel cut off, unable to say what waits to be said. "I strongly disagree. I don't believe in God."

He smiles at me, showing the patience and compassion that has always prevented me from disliking him. "God probably doesn't mind much, so I can't either."

I'm not sure if he's joking, but he smiles, so I do, too.

"The question is not what are you sorry for, Rachel. We are all sorry. The question is why are you sorry?"

"I—"

He holds his hand up to stop me. No one will let me confess! "Take your time, Rachel. Don't rush. Remember the old saying about the Lord? He may not be there when you need him, but when he gets there he's right on time."

"That certainly separates him from the Shilohans."

His mouth twitches and I think I've gone too far. Both of our attempts at humor have faltered. But his face rearranges, and he laughs, short and loud, leaning back and clasping his hands over the slightest bulge of a belly.

"You're always welcome here, Rachel."

PASSING THE DOOR to the church nursery on my way out, I see Tom and Lily at a play table, with animal crackers and coloring books.

"Hi horse lovers. What are you up to?" I ask from the doorway. Instead of answering, Lily holds up her picture, and I have no choice but to step inside the room.

"That's nice, Lily. You're a very good colorer."

"Yeah," she says, looking down at Noah and a few of his yellow and purple passengers. "I color *a lot.*"

Crouching down, at one of the play-table chairs so low my knees are halfway to my chest, I pat her arm and hand her a cracker.

"Do you always come here after school?" I ask, glancing at the clock on the wall.

"No," Tom says, "just today. I'm here to pick Lily up because her bus is earlier than mine."

"Are your parents home now?"

"Not yet. Grandma had to go to the hospital for some tests. But they'll be back soon."

"They went to the big hospital, where the baseball team is," Lily says. "And the devil school."

"Duke," Tom says. "They're the Blue Devils, Lily. The town is called Durham. They have special doctors there."

"Are you okay here?" I ask as I move toward the door.

Tom nods. "Let's go home and have a snack, Lily. Then they'll be back."

Lily lifts her wristwatch where Ronald McDonald points to four and twelve. "Can we go to your house?" she asks, giving me an alarmingly direct look.

"Oh," I say, fumbling for an excuse. "I don't—"

Tom gazes at me knowingly over his sister's head and I feel caught out and a bit ashamed. "Lily, let's go to our house. We're supposed to wait until they get home. They didn't say we could go anywhere else."

"But when will they be home?" she asks, pointing to the watch.

"Soon," Tom answers, and Lily grimaces in frustration, squinching her eyes closed and squeezing a crayon in each hand. "I've got this watch and no one tells me what time I need to know," she mutters in a surprisingly adult tone.

"Have fun," I say, eager to get away. "Be careful."

AT HOME, I hack at the garden some more, and find myself huffing my grievances into the dirt. I just want to be alone. But one must be a member of the community. One must go along and get along. I look at the field and see the absurdity of my life here, I who don't even know how to weed a garden properly or when to plant what or how to drive a combine or whether corn and soybeans are possible to grow without degrading the land and spewing pesticides into the air.

I do not know how to connect, how to be a communitarian, and I don't want to. Yet I'm drawn here, at least the rent is paid, and I seem to be in love with Lyric. I strike the ground with the hoe and look at the dirt that reminds me how I cannot speak. I could never speak. I cannot even tell the parents of my dead friend what happened in his last moments. How can I live as a person in the world when I cannot even reconcile my own childhood?

Don't dwell, I tell myself, as I recklessly weed the garden. Don't dwell! I don't know how to garden. I never bothered to ask my mother. But everyone knows weeds have to be pulled out by the roots. I'm clearing the entire plot with wild hoe strikes when I'm interrupted by the sound of a truck tearing down the road. I glance up to see Tobias's Ram, coming toward me like the red eye of a dust tornado.

I straighten, taking in my sun hat and my plastic boots, amused at myself, the picture of a local landowner. Before I can comprehend the sight, the truck fishtails into the driveway and Minister Swain emerges from the passenger side and runs toward me, clutching his hat to his chest, his face haggard as Saint Jerome's in the wilderness.

"Rachel! It's happened—again."

Tobias is gesturing through the open truck window with a bloody hand.

"No cell service," Minister Swain says, panting, and I think he's having a heart attack.

"Lily's been shot!" Tobias shouts.

"No!"

"Rachel, listen. Call 9-1-1 and tell them to meet us on 64. Tom needs to stay with you. Jefferson!" he shouts to Minister Swain, "I need you to hold Lily's neck. I've got to drive." This last part he shouts as he swerves into the grass and turns around. The truck is moving as Minister Swain jogs heavily toward the passenger door, which hangs open and awkward as a broken bone. I start running, too, as the words swarm around my head, unordered, senseless. *Lily! Ambulance! Shot!* It's as though I'm running in slow motion, along the bottom of a pool. Minister Swain is gripping the door and heaving himself into the moving truck. His right foot with its white sock and orthopedic shoe dangles for a heartbreaking moment before it is pulled inside. The door closes and the foot is gone. Tom, who must have gotten out at Tobias's command, is standing beside the driveway like a phantom.

I run toward the house, then back toward Tom, then toward the house again. On the kitchen phone, I try to speak slowly and coherently, saying the words no one wants to say, that a five-year-old has been shot. Outside, Tom is still as a bloody scarecrow. Red fingerprints streak his face where he has wiped tears and evidence. I kneel before him and reach for his hands.

"Tom, what happened?"

He looks at me, as though focusing for the first time. His silence is terrifying.

"You don't have to say anything."

He shakes his head. "I was in charge," he whispers. "I thought it wasn't loaded."

"Why don't we sit in the grass and wait?"

"Wait for what?"

"To hear how Lily is."

"Is she going to heaven?"

"Not yet, I hope."

As we sit side by side looking at this lonely place, I see a red wolf—it *is* a red wolf—beyond the house at the edge of the woods. He is looking at us, a coppery figure under the darker brownish copper of the tree trunks. He sees us.

Tom lies on his back in the grass and moves his arms and legs, making an angel though there is no snow. I gesture silently, pointing toward the wolf. Tom lifts his head, looks, lowers his head back to the ground.

"Tell him to come," he says. "Tell that wolf to come eat me up."

"You stay right here with me. That wolf is not going to eat anybody."

"Then why is he here?"

"The wolf is watching over us. We're just going to lie here and hold on."

"Hold on to what?"

"The grass, the earth. Here, hold on to me."

I reach for his hand. It is small and warm and closed. He stares up at the sky as a tear trickles toward his ear, turning the fingerprint into a delicate pink bloom on his cheek. The vision rises before me of the lamb's blood above doors so the lord would pass over them and not smite the firstborns. There is no Passover. There are only guns and children killing one another.

Tom is crying noiselessly, like an adult. He doesn't pull his hand away to wipe his tears. He doesn't turn his head, even as the tears drip into his naked shell-shaped ears. I cannot comfort him.

Finally, he turns his head and speaks so softly I lean closer to hear.

"What if I killed Lily?"

I squeeze his hand.

"We have to wait."

We lie in the grass on the spinning earth and I look toward the coppery figure at the edge of the dark woods, *from whence cometh my help*. But the wolf only watches.

PART TWO

✦ ✦ ✦

STORY OF A SHOOTING

1985

NINE

THERE'S ALWAYS SOMEONE faring worse than you, my mother used to say, and she was always right.

My father's final word on suffering was not spoken at all. It was a summer day I think of as the summer of childhood, which has collapsed into one day in a long season. A bluejay with a broken neck was lying in the grass of the backyard. At first, he was upright, making odd twitchy movements. I thought he was caught on something; his body jerked up and down as though pulled on a wire by an unseen hand. Then he went over on his back, and I said, or was it Garland who said, "His neck is broken." "Poor thing," Professor said. It was awful, but we couldn't turn away. We crept closer. The bluejay's instinct was to fly off. He jumped and fluttered on his back under our watchful gaze.

I kept hoping he would go away, but he stayed there, alive and jerking and falling back to the ground all afternoon.

Mom told us not to look. But the three of us kept drifting back to the spot, watching the bird in the grass. Hours later, he was still thrashing and dying his slow, violent death. When our father came in from the field, he sat in the folding lawn chair to take off his boots. We observed him in the silent solemnity we had acquired that afternoon.

"What's ailing you?"

Garland and I didn't answer, instinctively shielding the bird from our father's rejection of slow ends. Professor, trusting and obedient, pointed to the spot where the bird thrashed.

"How long has it been there?"

"Hours and hours," Professor said.

"His neck is broken," I said quickly in explanation, glaring at Professor, who had innocently issued a death warrant.

"Rachel, bring him here."

Why hadn't he asked Garland, who lifted his chin challengingly to me? He couldn't have refused either, but he could act tough now that I was chosen to fetch the dying creature.

"I don't want to touch him," I protested.

"Bring him here. He won't hurt you. He's afraid."

I stepped into the grass, feeling the soft, cool blades under my bare feet. Garland watched from the porch, and Professor followed behind me. I moved reluctantly toward the bluejay. He was still jumping, but lower now, with longer bouts of recovery. As I stood over him, he tried to fly away, but hit the ground again. I squatted beside him, speaking quietly, telling him I was going to pick him up. He fluttered in fear and I jumped. There were no voices from the porch, but I felt my father's eyes on my back. Garland's, too. Professor was a few feet behind me, at a close but safe distance. I bent toward the bird. When

I felt his feathers, I dropped him. I turned and looked at my father, hoping he would let me return to the house. But he nodded in that way he had, *Go ahead, do as you're told.* So I covered the bluejay with my hand and scooped him up, walking fast through the grass, passing Professor and holding the jay out in front of me, with his broad blue and white tail sticking out from my cupped palms.

I handed him to my father, who, with barely a movement, took the bluejay and twisted his neck nearly off. Then he handed him back to me, and I automatically accepted the bird, because if my father handed you something, you took it.

"What do I do with it?"

Professor approached us ashen faced, shocked speechless.

"Toss it over by the woods. Then wash your hands."

Act. Be done. Don't dwell.

I did as he said, taking the bird to the edge of the woods, but I couldn't throw it on the ground, instead staring at the dead bird in my quivering hand. Professor crouched beside me and began making a small coffin-nest of pinestraw and pin oak leaves. He took the bird gently and arranged him carefully in his grave. My father had gone inside; Garland watched as Professor and I approached the porch, holding hands.

"Judas," Garland hissed at me.

"Dad told me to."

"Judas," he said, for the second and final time.

He took off to his brooding spot in the deer stand, where I was forbidden.

In the morning, the bluejay was gone; only two dark feathers lay on his leafy grave.

I WAS THE one who wanted to hunt the ghost. It was a few months after the death of the bluejay, and a warm fall night like any other except that we (Garland, Professor, and me) were sneaking out of the house in the hot dark to take the trail through the woods, as we so often did in the daytime. We had to go at night to find the ghost of Joe Brooks.

We waited until midnight, when our parents had been inaudible for an hour, and went out the window. We liked to think we were getting away with something, even though our parents were pure tired and only cared that we were quiet. We had never snuck out of the house before. In fact, Garland, who was twelve to my eleven, had begun to ignore me and pull away from our games. I wanted back in his good graces, and was driven by dares. I had smoked the most cigarettes behind the barn, snatching the tenth and final one from the pack a visitor had forgotten at Professor's house. My parents, the teetotal tobacco farmers, didn't smoke. I had inhaled quickly, blowing in Garland's face and gloating over my victory. Then I heaved in the grass while Garland said it served me right.

"It doesn't mean anything anyway," he said.

"It means plenty," I retorted, as reflux burned my smoky throat. "It means I won."

I was also enjoying a little local fame after eating a tobacco worm. Garland had warned me not to do it, but he warned me away from everything. Tobacco worms were easy to find on the ground, where they glinted like shards of green glass. We had different ways of killing: pulling them in half, drowning them in kerosene, stomping them to death, or throwing them against the barn post, where they left a wet mark against the wood. They thumped and splattered, and we danced around their remains, singing in deathly delight: "Nobody likes me / everybody hates me / Think I'll go eat worms."

I had managed not to heave when I ate the worm, which was tough and nubby and thick as a man's finger. "Long thin skinny ones / short fat juicy ones / Watch them wriggle and squirm."

So I was a seeker of dares that night when I was eleven and Professor was eleven minus a month and Garland was twelve and starting to shun us. I had come up with the scare dare: the nighttime hunt for Joe Brooks. Garland brought his gun. He had gotten it for his birthday four months earlier, and he took it everywhere. I argued that you can't use a gun on a ghost, but I was just jealous. I loved guns and wanted one of my own. It was one more thing for boys only. I watched with envy as Garland carefully wrapped the rifle in a pillowcase and dropped it from my window.

He twisted the napkin full of bullets so they wouldn't jangle and put them in his pocket. Then he jumped from the window, moved the rifle with his foot, and held out his hand to help me. I ignored him and jumped the few feet to the ground, with my arms out, trying to stick the landing like Mary Lou Retton. It was a nearly full moon, and the pale dirt road glowed and beckoned like a worry bone. Professor was waiting for us at the stop sign. He was tamping the dirt with his sandal, and looked at us through his black frame glasses, his eyes frightened and alert. We called him Professor because he read constantly, more than Garland, more than me even, and more than anyone we knew. His father, Minister Swain, had come by a set of *World Book Encyclopedia*, with mixed emotions. Professor was determined to read his way through it, and was allowed as long as he kept up with his Bible lessons. He was trying to hit the Aztecs before Vacation Bible School.

"How far to find the ghost?"

"You're not going to start are you, Rachel? If you whine, I won't take you."

I felt goose bumps on my arms, and I knew they looked like plucked poultry because I was a big chicken. But Garland wasn't to know. "Let's go then, Evil, if we got to walk to Mississippi." As North Carolinians, we thought Mississippi was the end of the world.

"Are you going to shoot it?" Professor asked, looking at the gun.

"It's for protection."

"I don't think you can shoot a spirit. I mean, they're already dead."

"Why don't you two smarties stay home?" Garland said. "I'll go myself."

"No way." I was willing to do anything to close the gap that was opening between Garland and me. Professor, I bossed mercilessly. He liked my recklessness, and I liked that he caused me to stop and think, even as he was a loyal servant to my schemes.

The road ran straight as an unending row between the sun-hardened fields. I really thought it ran all the way to Mississippi, like the trains that passed Spivey's Crossroads with the big white block letters spelling s-o-u-t-h-e-r-n. *Southern Serves the South*, I would sing along with the man on the radio. *Southern gives the green light to in-no-vat-ion.*

"Come on, little bookworms," Garland said.

We entered the woods by the old stick barn, with its earthy smell of wood and tobacco and the dark dirt of the floor that

I swept with a leaf broom. We had played there all our child-hoods. The burners were spaced evenly along metal pipes, and before the barn was filled and locked and gassed, I used the cold burners to cook weed and snakeberry stews for Professor and some imaginary friends. Snakeberry was poisonous, which I had forced Professor to find out the hard way when we were in kindergarten. He had only been sick for three days, and, to our disappointment, hadn't needed the hospital in Greenvale.

We walked the woods, Garland with his gun and me with a cattail sword and Professor empty-handed.

"Onward Christian sol-diers," we sang softly, the only marching song we knew. "Marching as to war. With the cross of Je-e-sus, Going on before."

We passed the hunting camp, as we had done many times in daylight, and turned toward the swamp. It was the Little Dismal, not the Great Dismal, which was somewhere else where they had great things.

"Come on," Garland said, waving the flashlight. "Hurry up!"

"Let me hold the gun. You can't carry both."

"Rachel, do like I say so Joe Brooks won't get you."

"Just let me carry it. It's slowing you down."

"You're slowing me down! Jesus H. Christ."

We went on for a while, Garland first, because he was old-est, he was tallest, and that was his place. I followed close behind.

"Slow down, please," Professor called from the rear. "I got rocks in my shoes."

I turned back to see the outline of his white T-shirt crumple as he bent over to empty his shoe.

He ran to catch up, bumping into me and scaring himself. I reached out and ran my hand over his buzz cut that I loved to touch, soft and giving as summer grass.

"Jesus H. Christ!"

We continued behind Garland, who was not only first, but carried the flashlight and the gun.

"What's the 'H' for?"

Professor giggled and slapped me on the back. He was my best friend and would do anything I told him to. I had already baptized him—twice—in the swimming hole.

"Haywood."

"Rachel!" Garland shout-whispered. "You are aggravation."

He turned and tried to shove me, but his hands were full. "Be careful with that gun, Garland. Did you take the bullets out?"

"I think so." He paused. "I always do."

"You know what Dad said about safety." Dad had taken us both to learn to shoot. He had me draw a target on the cardboard box, a stick figure with a huge smiley face because that's the best I could do.

"The safety's on," Garland said. "But I ought to take it off and blow your brains out."

"Then we'd have two ghosts, and I would haunt you and scare the mess out of you. So, boo!"

"Boo Radley!" Professor shouted. We had read the Reader's Digest condensed version of *To Kill a Mockingbird* three times together and never missed an opportunity to quote from it. The mention of Boo Radley, or, our favorite *Mockingbird* word, *chiffarobe*, sent us into ecstasy.

"Professor, sugar, did you put my *chiffon* dress in the *chiffarobe*?"

"Sugar, I've looked all over tarnation, but I can't find your *chiffon* dress in the *chiffarobe*!"

We fell against each other in word-drunk delight.

"I can't believe I'm stuck with you two nutty book nerds," Garland said. "Now shush, and let's get to Big Beech Island. Not that anything will be there now. I'm sure you've scared off the ghosts, the frogs and the crickets, and every living thing."

"Please, Garland. Let me hold the gun. Pretty please."

He ignored me, and we started off again, Professor with his hand on my shoulder so we could stay together in the dark.

"And be ye kind one to another," I sang. It was the tune that always got to Garland. "Tenderhearted, forgiving one another, even as God for Christ's sake hath forgiven you. Da doo, doodle de doo, E-phe-sians 4:32."

"Rachel, if I let you carry the gun, will you be quiet and behave?"

"I'll try."

He handed me the gun, and I felt its weight. It was a beautiful rifle; a Winchester 70 that my father had bought from a landlord whose tenant left it for rent money. It was a collector's item, and it was Garland's.

"About that 'H,'" Professor said.

"Hanfield."

"Harvey."

"Hortense."

"That's for a gir—"

"Shhhh," Garland whispered, and I bumped him as he stopped short.

"What is it?"

We were in the clearing of Big Beech Island, a stand of beech trees in the middle of the Little Dismal. Why do they call it an island? I had asked Garland many times. It isn't a real island. Why do they call you Rachel? he replied. It's just a name.

"Quiet!"

We all heard it, the sound somewhere in front of us.

Professor took my hand. "Is it Joe Brooks?"

"Shh!"

We crept forward, keeping close, toward the terrible sound. My hand sweated on the gun as Garland shined the flashlight, first on the eerie gray of beech bark and then lower, on a mound of lumpy fur. Professor whimpered.

"What is it?"

Antlers lifted from the middle of the beast, two tired skinny deer, lying on their bellies, their bodies in opposite directions and their heads together in the middle.

"What's wrong with them?"

"They got their antlers locked."

The three of us huddled in awe and fright.

"How'd they get like that?"

"Rutting," Garland said.

"What's rutting?"

"Women," Garland said with disgust.

"But what's rutting?"

"Means they were fighting over some doe and they knocked their antlers together and got stuck."

The deer bowed their heads in shame. One of them made a peeping sound.

"Maybe they were just playing," I protested, "like boys do."

"Girls are trouble, Professor," Garland said. "Remember that."

He continued to shine the light on the deer where they lay. Their bellies were bloated but their ribs showed, flabby balloons in bone cages.

"How long have they been here?" Professor whispered.

"Long enough to get skinny."

"Go up there, Garland," I said, "and unstick them."

"It's too late."

"No." I moved toward the deer. They were pitiful up close, but also scary, because they were near death.

"They're suffering, Garland. Dad said we shouldn't let things suffer."

"When did he say that?"

"We better go back," Professor said.

I crept closer toward the dying beast with two heads. "Shine the light steady, Garland."

"Stop, Rachel."

Garland grabbed my arm, but I shook him off.

"Be careful," I said. "The gun."

"You be careful, you."

"You be careful," I mimicked.

As I crouched before the deer, they began to struggle, weakly. Everything was different now. I was in the middle, between Garland and Professor and the dying deer, and I stood up straight, clutching the gun.

"Rachel, don't be dumb. Come back!"

With my next step something moved behind me, and one deer, or maybe both melded as one, screamed. Hunters said they could scream, but I had never heard it myself. It was the sound of being alone in the woods at night and seeing a ghost.

"Rachel!"

"That one's neck is broken," I said, pointing the gun.

"Come back," Professor said. I had forgotten he was there. "Rachel," he said, pleadingly. I hated that sniffy way he had of begging and whining.

The boys were coming closer behind me. The deer were making sounds I couldn't bear. The one with the broken neck was crying as the other one raised his head, and twelve antlers rose like a crown of bony thorns. Professor seized my hand.

"Get back!"

I took the safety off and raised the rifle. I heard my father saying, "Don't pull the trigger. Just squeeze it gently, like a spongeful of water over a baby's head."

"Rachel! Don't you do it."

How many times had Garland said those words? Don't do this. Don't do that.

"It's not loaded is it?" Professor was panicking, his voice had that whimpering tone I hated, and he reached for me, but I shook him off. The sound from the deer was new and terrible. Something moved past me. Something screamed—me?—I squeezed the trigger.

I fell back with the recoil. Garland scrambled in front of me, and then he was lying on top of the deer that were suddenly shrouded in Professor's T-shirt. It wasn't his shirt. It was—

"Professor!" I shouted. "Get up right now Rufus Swain!"

I flung myself on top of Garland, who lay on the mound of fur and blood. He pushed me back so roughly I fell. As I tried to rise, he jumped on me, holding me down, pinning my arms wide.

The deer gave a terrible moan, like nothing I had ever heard. Garland's cowboy belt buckle was digging into my stomach.

"Get off me!"

We turned back to the pitiful pile. The deer were drawing their last breaths. Professor was lying on his back on top of them, spilling blood from his chest.

"Professor, get up!"

We crouched over our friend. Garland looked at me and shook his head.

"Rachel," he said. "Run."

"But—"

"Run! Now!"

"Garland—"

"Get help, Rachel. I'll stay here. Go!"

He handed me the flashlight and I took off through the woods. I looked back once, into the dark, and I couldn't see, but I could hear the deer breathing. Was it the deer breathing? I turned back toward the trees, and felt a wind blow through my body. It was Joe Brooks. I knew it was Joe Brooks and that he was coming for me and that I deserved to die.

The ghost was at my back now, pouncing, pulling me to the ground. I fell, face down, waiting to die. Instead, a thick warm tongue licked the back of my neck. I lifted my head and a red wolf was standing over me. I didn't scream. I didn't make a sound. He looked at me with his golden eyes like stones at the bottom of a clear stream. It was almost a stream I could step into. He leaned down and nudged my arm, then he was gone.

MY PARENTS WERE UP, waiting. They'd woken, and discovered we were gone. Dad was preparing to go in search of us, figuring we hadn't gone far. The light was on in the living room, and they were in the kitchen, the room where everything happened. Mom had just made coffee and was pouring the steaming dark sludge into Dad's silver thermos. She turned and looked at me through the kitchen's arched doorway. I could tell my father was in the room with her before I entered. When he saw my face his look changed from anger to fear, a shadow crossing his sharp features. I stood in the middle of the room, opening and closing my mouth like a fish. He held me by the shoulders.

"Is Garland with you?"

I couldn't speak. The vinyl tablecloth covered the kitchen table, hanging longer on one end.

"Do you have something to tell me, Rachel?"

"Big Beech Island," I whispered.

He shook me, and I started to cry. "A wolf."

"Did you see something?"

"A wolf."

"There are no wolves," he said, shaking me hard. "Think. Where's Garland?"

"Rachel," my mother said and looked at my father. She wrung a damp dishtowel in her hands, a cloth wall calendar from 1974. "She's in shock."

"Is he hurt?" My father said, striding toward the door.

"Professor," I said, and started to cry. "I thought he was the deer."

"Leith," my mother said, wrapping the cloth around her hand like a mitt. "Shouldn't you take Rachel?"

My father paused, looking at me as I hid my hands under the table, rubbing the edge of the checked tablecloth.

"Rufus is hurt, but Garland is with him, on Beech Island?"

I nodded, and he was gone. My mother wanted to be angry with me, but she was also worried, so she took it out on 1974, my birth year, wrapping the rough towel of the past in her hands.

"Do you have something you want to tell me?" she asked, repeating his words. When we had done something wrong, we could usually be counted on to confess.

"Why do they call it an island?"

"What?"

"It's not a real island."

My bewildered mother worried about my mind then, and she draped the dishtowel over my shoulders, as though shrouding me, or swaddling me, in the past. I pressed my face into the table, rubbing my sweaty cheek against the blue tablecloth. My mother took my hand, and we prayed. She prayed to God, and I prayed to the wolf.

TWO POLICEMEN CAME to the house to question us. I repeated the story exactly as I had been instructed. We were ghost hunting. Garland had taken his gun to protect us. He thought it wasn't loaded, but there was one forgotten cartridge. We came upon the dying deer and felt bad for them. They were suffering. Garland shot them, out of pity, but Professor had tried to save them at the last minute by dashing forward and covering the deer with his body.

"Did he say anything?" the policemen asked.

"No."

"Did Garland see him?"

"No."

"Was it dark?"

"Yes, very dark. We only had a flashlight."

"So it was very dark and you couldn't see. Did you understand what was happening?"

"It happened fast."

"I'm sure it did."

"They were suffering," I said again. "We're not supposed to let things suffer."

"No, of course not," one cop agreed, looking down at his hat, which he turned slowly in his hands.

"Aren't you ashamed?" Mom said to him. "Questioning children like this."

They had trouble looking at us then, looking instead at the walls and the cross-stitched prayer hanging above the television. *God grant me the serenity to accept the things I cannot change* . . .

"We won't be long."

The one who spoke stood with his big feet planted wide. "It's just my job."

The younger one looked at the wall. *Courage to change those things we can* . . .

"It was a mistake," Mom said. Dad moved to her and tried to take her hand but she snatched it away, and moved behind Garland, her hands on his shoulders. "My son made a mistake." Garland looked at us then, searching our faces as though we were strangers.

And wisdom . . .

"It was an accident!" I cried. "It was—" My father held my hand, the first and last time I remember him doing so. I looked at the grotesque appendage and saw that it belonged to me. Mom sank down on the couch and began to cry and we stood over her, dry-eyed and useless.

TEN

MY FATHER WAS not charged, because that wasn't done, not here, not then. They prayed about it at church, and I opened my eyes to look at Minister Swain and his wife as Deacon Chase named my family, one by one, praying for our souls and our guidance and for the police, too, that they would see the error of imposing man's law on a tragic situation best left to God.

Sometime after Professor's funeral, Dad took Garland into the woods with the rifle. They had target practice, day after day after day, just the two of them. Garland hated it, but he did as my father instructed, dutifully, and never forgave us.

WE WERE NEVER punished for that night, but for a while we were in trouble all the time. There was something running underneath with our father, a cord of tension that was always taut, but I wouldn't understand until years later. I was not girl-ish enough to be a girl; Garland was not boyish enough to be a boy. Not in our father's eyes. He couldn't understand people at all except with the sharpest distinctions between women and men. Garland and I couldn't be other than what we were, either, just a couple of kids, confused and unfree.

I began to feel wild, and goaded Garland with risks and dares, until Dad found out about our smoking contests behind the barn. I had won again, and was euphoric for the first time since Professor's death.

"Your father wants to see both of you right now," Mom said one afternoon, as we banged into the house.

We followed her into the kitchen. Garland turned to me and mouthed, "Did you tell? You told."

No, I shook my head, and zipped my index finger across my lips.

We stood in the archway, watching him at the head of the dining table.

"Do you have something to tell me, Garland?"

"No, sir."

In the kitchen corner his wingtips sat on the polish-splattered newspaper, worn but shined and waiting for Sunday.

"Sit down."

Garland pulled his chair out, and, realizing it was going to scrape the floor, he stopped and squeezed his skinny body into the seat. I very carefully lifted my chair away from the table and perched.

"I said, Do you have something to tell me, son?"

"No, sir."

"Dad, I—"

"Rachel," he said, and looked at me for the first time. "Were you spoken to?"

"No, sir."

He struck the first match against his thumbnail.

"Leith," Mom said from the doorway, as we all watched the match burn.

"If Garland is going to smoke, he should learn to do it properly," he said without turning. He lifted the cigarette to his mouth and lit it just as the fire reached his nail. I had never seen him smoke before, although he did it with a kind of rigid accuracy.

"Smoking at the barn they're liable to set the whole farm on fire."

Garland didn't look at me but kicked me under the table. I refused to cry out and squeezed my eyes shut. *I didn't tell, Garland.* I repeated this to myself and concentrated so Garland would know. We used to be able to talk like that. During long church sermons I would think thoughts and he would write down what they were and we would trade.

Dad breathed in slow and deep. There was only the sound of his dry lips parting before he held the cigarette out for Garland. "Go ahead."

Garland's raised hand seemed to float above the table, a dismembered hand with long slim fingers, faint traces of dirt under his nails, a few snags of skin near his cuticles. He took the cigarette, trying not to touch Dad's fingers. He was very stiff as he took a small puff.

"You can do better than that."

"But Dad, it's my fault. I'm the one—"

"Rachel, no one is talking to you. Now hush."

"Leith," Mom said again from the doorway.

Garland glared at Dad and took a hard defiant drag. He

tried to swallow a cough but sputtered, then inhaled deeper to hide his humiliation.

"I didn't tell, Garland. I promise."

The smoking contest had been my idea. I was the one who swiped the pack from Jackson's Grocery, while the men stood around gossiping and shaking their pocket change. Garland turned to me with narrowed eyes and blew smoke in my face. I opened my mouth to catch it but he didn't care.

Dad lit the next cigarette and held it between his thumb and index finger. "Don't let this burn a hole in your mother's tablecloth."

Garland stubbed his cigarette out in the abalone ashtray mom kept in the sewing closet for company. He wouldn't look at any of us. He stared glassy-eyed through the smoke, toward the kitchen window, where the thin yellow curtains breathed with the breeze.

"Son?" Mom took a step toward his chair. No one responded. I looked at her and understood that this was a boy's game and we could only watch. Dad lit the next match before Garland could finish; the flame burned blue above his thumb.

"Do you have anything to tell me?"

"No, sir."

Halfway through the pack Garland rested his head on his arms and the cigarette shook in his hand. He dropped it in the ashtray and pushed away from the table.

"Sit down."

He tried to run out of the kitchen but banged into the wall like a blind man.

"Leave him," Mom said, her eyes flashing bright as a flare.

I stood up and moved near Garland, who was leaning against the wall.

"It was *me!*" I cried.

Dad stood, his chair at the head of the table falling behind him. "Garland, sit down."

"You're the one who grows it!" I yelled, but no one responded.

He moved toward us, his hand raised, and I stepped in front of Garland. He caught himself just in time.

"Don't ever stand in front of your brother again," he said, as Garland ran from the room and out of the house.

I FOUND HIM at the Red Dredge swimming hole. His shoes and shirt were flung along the bank, but I kept mine on, and waded to where he stood, breathing heavy and wiping the water from his eyes.

"Show me how to float, Garland."

"I don't want to."

"Come on," I said, grabbing his hands, and holding his arms out. He didn't move or protest, so I put my hands around his neck and hoisted myself into his arms.

"I don't want to," Garland whispered as he held me afloat.

"Don't want to what?"

"It wasn't my fault," he said, and I pulled away, but he tightened his grip.

"Dad said—"

"We have to say it was me because it's my gun. But it wasn't."

"I know. I'll tell. I'll say it. I'll tell everybody."

"It's too late. Nobody'd believe you."

"Can I tell you a secret, Garland? That night, when I was running through the woods, a red wolf was chasing me. I fell down, and he caught me, but he didn't hurt me. He licked and nuzzled. He was like a wolf angel. Do you think it could have been Professor?"

Garland's face went dark. "What's wrong with you? You didn't see a wolf. They're extinct. Everybody knows that. Grow up, Rachel. You can't live forever in a fairy tale."

He looked down at me; I was on my back, held close in his arms. It was the only time in my life I was afraid of him. I squirmed but he held me fast.

"You're so light in the water, Rachel," he said less harshly. "You know how the preacher says we're supposed to be ready to die every day. You know how Abraham takes Isaac to Mount Moriah, and is going to sacrifice him?"

"At the last minute God tells him to kill the ram instead. He doesn't kill Isaac."

"But he would have! Do you think Isaac ever trusted him again?" He gives me a wild-eyed, wrathful look that I cannot understand on Garland's face. "What if you were Isaac and I was Abraham?" he says, gripping me tighter.

"I can't be Isaac. I'm a girl. What if you were Isaac and Dad was Abraham?"

"If Dad was Abraham I'd already be dead."

ELEVEN

OUR TIME OF trouble never ended. First, we stopped talking to one another, because we were a family of not talking, not telling. Then Garland began to hate me, and finally the deer hunt severed our relationship entirely.

It was a few months after Professor's death, and Mom was glad when the three of us agreed to go hunting together. She packed fried chicken and biscuits in a paper sack, and Garland held it to his nose, smiling at her. He took it outside first, packing food before guns.

We were silent in the truck and I thought of the three-day ride Isaac made with Abraham. But if Dad was Abraham and Garland was Isaac, who was I? Isaac had no sister. Dad was staring straight ahead as though the road was streaming from his eyes. He pulled over near the baseline road. Before we entered the woods, he stood and raised his arms to the sky.

Garland didn't want me in his deer stand, but Dad told him to take me.

"Be careful," he said. "Remember our review."

We had been over and over gun safety since Professor's death. We had reviewed it when Garland first got the gun, but after the funeral, it became a daily ritual. Dad sat on the beige carpet of the living room floor, making each of us load and unload the rifle, the shotgun, the double barrel, the pistol, put the safety on and count the cartridges. It was not grim, but brisk, almost professional, and I hated it. I knew Garland did, too, but he wouldn't look at me. We were careful and when we had mastered the movements, we went faster. Garland, who had always been methodical, made sure he was faster than me, and I went faster to keep up. "Slow down," Dad said, as he stood and watched. He never sat when we were loading the guns. He stood over us, looking down with his grave expression from church when he stood at the end of the row waiting for the communion cups to be passed down the pew.

THE DEER STAND was new and Garland preferred his old one. There was a small clearing near Beech Island, and a lone dogwood had grown near the common trees, mostly pine, with the occasional sweet gum and maple and hickory. This stand was one of the new plastic models, ready-made, suspended in the tree like the single seat of a Ferris wheel that had been flung off, and had flown through the sky, settling in the tree branches. There was even a bar that came down in front so we wouldn't fall out.

I climbed up the tree ladder first and made room for Garland, who settled beside me unhappily, taking up more space than he needed. We started to jostle each other, but Garland put on his serious face and hugged his side of the seat, brought the bar down and ignored me. We sat in the tree, with Dad nearby, our man on the ground. After about ten minutes I reached for the food sack, and Garland glared at me as the bag rustled.

I put the bag down, which was hard; I wanted a biscuit. But I was determined to be quiet, because Garland was letting me stay close. He rocked his bright orange hat back and forth on his head, and I imitated him. Then I sat beside my brother and did not say anything and did not reach for food, nor did I touch the rifle between us, but sat looking down through the leaves that seemed to breathe with us in the hush, until I felt Garland's hand on my arm and thought I might fall from the tree I was so happy.

"Shhhh." He pointed below, where a deer nibbled at the leaves of a mulberry tree. It raised its head, and I held my breath. That was my favorite part, when a deer stopped dead still and lifted its head, while the whole world waited. The deer seemed to look at us, its mouth full but not chewing.

"He sees us."

"Don't move," Garland whispered.

The deer went back to chewing. Garland put his finger to his lips, and lifted the rifle to his shoulder. Nothing happened. He looked through the scope, but didn't move.

"Take the shot," I whispered.

The deer looked up once, then turned, and his white tail disappeared through the shaking leaves so fast it was as though he was never there.

Garland's face reddened, as he lowered the rifle, tight to his side.

"If you say one more word, I'll shove you out of this tree."

"I'm sorry."

He shook his head and got a biscuit from the bag. He didn't offer me one, but chewed angrily, looking straight ahead. I tried to be quiet and thought of what I had learned from the deer hunter's almanac. That deer are mostly mute and live their entire lives within a square mile. The book also said deer are color-blind, and I spent a long time thinking of how they might have discovered this.

I looked over at Garland, my brother, and at the leaves above and below, and everything was flowing and fresh and there was nothing to fear. I was with Garland in the trees and all was good again. I wanted to sing, but the song that came into my head was "Onward Christian Soldiers." That brought it all back. Something moved below, and I saw again the two deer with their antlers locked just as they were that night, a wasted and monstrous three-headed creature. As they lifted their heads with pain and effort, Professor was joined with them.

Garland elbowed me and pointed. A deer was below, chewing leaves. I couldn't see it well enough to tell if it was the same one, but glimpsed its fur through the leaves that were fluttering, showing their silver bottoms. Garland raised the rifle and looked at me. He was afraid I would speak and ruin his chance. I could tell by the stern look on his face he was daring me to make a sound. I stared back. *I won't make a peep, Garland. I promise.*

He looked through the scope, his movements hurried. Dad had told us not to rush. I wanted to speak! Hold it tight to your body, Garland. Focus on your target. Squeeze the trigger. *Squeeze it gently, like a spongeful of water over a baby's head.* But Garland was gripping the rifle tightly and moving it up and down. *Spongeful spongeful baby baby*. I leaned over and caught a glimpse of fur as Garland fired. There was a sound of fleeing, hooves against the dry forest floor. We saw then that it was a doe, not a buck, not what he wanted. I was relieved she got away.

"You rushed me," Garland said with hate in his voice. "I shot a doe."

"No. I was just—"

He scrambled down and walked away, toward my father, whose footsteps shuffled closer through the leaves.

"What happened?"

"I nicked a doe, but she ran off."

"Let's find her."

"She's a doe!"

"Does are fine. We haven't killed a doe this year. We've got four tags."

"Why did we have to bring Rachel? She is ruination."

Dad tried to speak kindly, but we recognized the irritation in his voice. "Come on. She probably didn't get far. Where's the wound?"

"Her flank."

Dad was squatting under the tree where the deer had been eating. We stood over him, not looking at each other. "She might be close."

We followed him through the woods. When we were gathered at the kitchen table that awful night, and my father said Garland would take the blame for Professor's death, I had asked why. Weren't we supposed to tell the truth? Yes, my father said, almost always, except on rare occasions. This was one of those. It was Garland's rifle, he said, and so it was right that Garland take responsibility. People would understand better. Understand what better? I had asked. It was me. It was my fault. Boys have guns, my father said. Sometimes accidents happen. It would be harder for people to understand about you. Because I'm a girl? It's better if we stop talking about this, Rachel. Stop dwelling on it.

We could not find Garland's wounded deer, the crippling loss. These woods were full of them. They could see us, and we could not see them.

AFTER HE WOUNDED the doe, Garland began to run away for short periods, a rehearsal for years later. Dad would let him stay out in the woods for hours, until midnight or so, and then he would go get him. I would watch from my bedroom window as the men, the hunters, went searching, the white from their flashlights bouncing through the woods like giant fireflies. They brought Garland back a prisoner. He sat up front, three more men squeezed in the cab of the truck that smelled like stale bloody hunting clothes stuffed behind the seat.

Garland stopped speaking to us. He stopped eating. He looked down at his plate. He looked down all the time. In my room I knocked on the wall, but he didn't answer. I watched from my window as our father moved up and down the rows of the field like a ghost who has lost his grave. Garland took refuge in his favorite deer stand near Beech Island, and when I followed he would say harshly, "Go on. Go on home," the same words in the same tone my father used with stray dogs.

Those are the words I think of when I think of Garland's voice. I should have fallen on my knees and told him I would confess to the town if he would take me back as a sister. But I did not, and he did not.

LATE AT NIGHT, when they went in search of him, I would sneak up to the attic, for a higher view, but I could not make out much beyond the garden, where a lonely hoe wore Dad's threadbare shirt. Lying on the attic floor, I thought of everyone below me, while I floated above. Garland would come back to us. Professor, never. I bit my copper bracelets. Some of the hunting tags said antlers. Some said antlerless. Antlers were much more valued.

I wanted to be the witch who sheds her skin, and flies over the land, keeping watch over the spirits, making friends with the wolf. *Skin, skin, you know me?* The witch, the deer, the crippling loss, Joe Brooks, and the wolf were all in the woods, bodies in flight. Mom and I, the women, were closed away in the dark and silent house, put away for the night, just sheet-covered shapes, while outside, the men hunted for Garland.

IN THE MORNING Garland would be at breakfast, as though nothing had happened.

I wanted to talk, but he wouldn't listen. He turned his hatred on me; I turned my hatred on our father. My mother was left out. She didn't truck in hate. She was a farmer's wife; when blight was brought, she shouldered it. We simply stopped being a family, and we lived together for years that way, strangers under the same roof.

I stopped working in the field. First I was embarrassed and

then I was ashamed and later I was embarrassed for being ashamed.

During the day there was school. Garland remained in the county system through high school, but I was allowed to go to the city district in Greenvale. Garland wanted me to go, which is probably why my father allowed it. The rules of my transfer were understood. I was not told to keep a high A average, but if I came home with a 98, I was reminded that was two short of 100.

Those were my days. At night there was the scrubbing, the constant struggle to rid myself of the soil, or the feel of it. Dirt hid in ears, inside elbows, behind knees, in dark delicate choker lines around the neck. It was embedded in fingernails and the lines of palms. The soil was in us. That's what made us different from people in other places. So I scrubbed, every night until the water ran clear. I scrubbed.

PART THREE

INHERITANCE

Late September 2015

TWELVE

THERE! ANOTHER DEAD wolf lies a few feet behind the garden, a fluffy rabbit tail protruding from its death-locked jaws.

I'm beginning to doubt myself. If there are fewer than forty red wolves in all of North Carolina, it's very unlikely that I've found two in three weeks.

It's hard to tell what killed it; apart from the vacant eyes, the wolf-thing looks full-furred, healthy, and ready to run. Sinking into the grass beside the animal, I want to stroke its head, but I shouldn't. My parents warned us many times: *If it's not afraid of you, don't touch. If it's acting strange, don't touch. If it's dead, don't touch.*

I think of Ernest's coyote lecture at the bar, and try to remember about the canid controversy. Endangered red wolves have been reintroduced into the wild in three counties, including this one. Farmers and locals hate being told how to preserve their land by "the state," whose enforcers, in truth, don't always understand the ecological web of small localities. At one town meeting I read about, a farmer said he was no match for a red wolf, who was crafty, and a better hunter than any man he knew. And he knew some good hunters.

My wolf, or the thing that looks like a wolf, reclines in majestic silence in the grass. He is a beautiful animal, with no visible signs of injury. He lies with his eyes open, as though sleeping peacefully, except for the bunny tail hanging from his rigid mouth. I ignore my parents' old warning and sink down beside him to stroke his head, and wonder if they, too, are born with fontanels, or if it's only the human skull that is born soft and incomplete.

My call to the game warden includes one accidental hang-up and a long music-less hold, then a voice tells me someone will come take a look. I have no idea what to do with the creature in the meantime. If I leave him in the grass, coyotes or vultures might pick him clean or cart him away.

Standing by the kitchen phone, I watch the wolf, who looks as though he is napping in the shade of the possum oak. That's the best tree in the yard, and when I was growing up, it was the skinning tree. It was also where I liked to read. Once, when I was sitting with my book at the very edge of the shade, I became convinced that a deer, strung up and being bled before he was skinned, was still alive. His eyes were open, and I thought I could hear him breathe. My father was in the garden digging sweet potatoes. I told him the deer was not dead. He laughed, for which I suppose I never forgave him. He's dead as dead. Dead as a doorstop, my father said. He's looking at me, I protested. He can't see you, Rachel. But his eyes are open. Things die with their eyes open, he said. It takes the living to close them. Why don't you close them then? It hardly matters, he answered. He can't see.

I cover the wolf corpse with a tarp, and wheelbarrow him into the laundry room and tumble him into the freezer.

GREENVALE DAILY NEWS

LILY RAE LANGLEY, 5, OF SHILOH, passed away on September 13, 2015.

Lily was born on January 1, 2010. She attended kindergarten at Shiloh Elementary. Lily enjoyed playing with her brother, Tom, and her imaginary horse, Priscilla Lorraine. Lily was full of joy and light and will never be forgotten.

In addition to her brother, Tom, survivors include her mother, Tilly Langley, and her father, Burl "B.J." Langley, of Shiloh; her maternal grandmother, Irma Mae Moye, of Shiloh; her paternal grandparents, Dorothy "Dot" and William Mayhue Langley, of Shiloh; and many cousins and extended family members.

A funeral service will be held at 1 p.m. on September 20 in Shiloh Church of Christ, Reverend Jefferson Swain officiating. Family will receive friends at the church 11–12:30 before the service.

"She didn't pass away," I mutter. "She died!"

There is nothing more wrong in the world than an obit for a five-year-old. I sink down on the driveway with the newspaper, and absently sweep the rocks with my hand. She asked to come to my house and I said no. She asked to come here and I said no.

I'm still sitting in the drive repeating this to myself when Tobias comes toward me, crunching gravel with his boots.

"You've seen the paper," he says, glancing at the pulpy pages on the ground.

"It's not safe here."

"It's not safe anywhere, Rachel."

"That's a stupid argument."

"I don't want to argue. I just came to say we should go to the funeral together. I can pick you up."

"I can't."

"You're a farm owner now. There are duties, obligations."

"Don't lecture me, Tobias."

He leans down. "I'm not lecturing you, Rachel. I'm saying there's been a death in our town, and you're here, you're a part of this place whether you want to be or not. We need you at the funeral. Tom needs you. Who understands better than you?"

He only knows I was there that night years ago; he can't know the rest. A strange sensation races up and down my spine, of heat and then cool. It's similar to the night I was running through the woods where Professor lay dying, and the wind was at my back, and the ghost blew through me. Tiny rocks have imprinted on my palms, and I brush them off, looking toward the field. I am ashamed. It's the old shame of being soiled.

"It's not a good idea, Tobias."

"A funeral for a five-year-old is never a good idea," he says, his voice thick. "But the town has to turn out."

"We're the ones who killed her!"

"Rachel, it was an accident."

"Accident!" I cry, standing and shoving him in the chest. "You think guns are so good, here, come inside, take them!"

Instead of responding, he follows me into the house. June growls from the couch, and he speaks to her in a low, commanding voice. This is enough to win her affection, and he pats her head as she nudges strong encouragement. They stay in the living room while I storm through the house, collecting weapons.

"Here." I lay them out on the floor. "I don't want them near me. I don't want them near my niece."

Tobias tilts his head back as though confronting a challenge.

"Rachel, everyone here has a gun. You're not in the middle of a city. No one can get here fast enough to save you. We all look out for each other, but we also have to look out for ourselves."

"Save me from what, the boogermonster?"

"Could be a copperhead. I shot thirteen this summer. We're not all careless, Rachel. Giving away your guns won't help anything."

Being near guns has never made my life safer. I won't take up arms that could easily be turned against me.

"I'll ask someone else."

"I'll keep them for you. Maybe you'll reconsider."

"I won't."

I hand him the soft paper bag, heavy with bullets. He gathers the .22, the Remington lightweight, the Fox Sterlingworth, the Winchester.

"I'll have them if you change your mind."

He wraps them in an old blanket and takes them outside, laying them gently in his truck bed. They're not loaded, but he double-checks, taking his time, showing me he can be cautious. It's maddeningly beside the point.

"Rachel, the last time I saw Garland, he asked me to take his guns, too. That's when I knew something was wrong. He was working around the barn and I gave him some peaches. I don't know why; it was too early in the season. But he hadn't been around much. Having him home was a rare and happy occasion for your parents."

Giving up guns, even I know, is giving up the ghost. The Southern man's last act, to lay down arms.

"Why would he ask you?" Tobias was only a year older than Garland, but they'd never been close.

"I was a neutral party. Giving away his guns was announcing his death."

"He didn't give them all away."

"No, he kept his one. He had use for it."

"You could have done something. He wasn't giving his guns away for no reason."

"Don't you think that haunts me? You're not the only one who lives with guilt."

Instead of asking him what he knows of my guilt, I stand, waiting for him to leave.

"Lily never came to, the whole time, in the truck. She just lay in Jefferson's arms like a bloody angel," he says with a shaken look, and also a sorrowful one. "She was wearing pink plastic clogs with cherries on them. One kept slipping off, and Jefferson kept putting it back on with his huge, clumsy hands."

He looks at me with his hazel eyes, his eyelashes thick with unfallen tears, and I'm seized with a terrible and overwhelming desire to touch him, to take comfort. This makes me angry, and I turn away, avoiding his gaze.

"Those shoes were so stupid, so useless, so tiny," he says, grabbing my arm and turning me to face him. "And I was furious at whoever bought these clown clogs for a child who should be running outside in sturdy shoes." His mouth trembles and I make no move as he kisses me on the forehead. "I'll be here Sunday at noon to pick you up."

THERE ARE STILL the days to get through.

With a sickening curiosity, I open the freezer in the laundry room. The corpse is already rigid. The rabbit tail hanging from his mouth is stiff and gruesome, as though in death the wolf has metamorphosed into some strange new animal that has the likeness of a wolf but is a carnivorous creature from a fairy tale. *Oh, I was so frightened!* Red Riding Hood cried. *It was so dark inside the wolf's body!* I let the freezer door slam shut.

I WALK JUNE, roam the house, pick up and put down three, four, five books. Within an hour I've called a dog boarder, booked a flight, and packed a bag.

"Come on, June. I'll drop you on the way to the airport."

Being a member of the most agreeable species, she jumps into the back seat of the rental car ready to roll.

Don't dwell. People spend their whole lives here, within a square mile, like deer. But it's so easy to leave. I pull onto the one road out of town and blast Billie Holiday, "Trav'lin' Light." I'm leaving: the rental car windows are up, the doors are locked, the car is a cocoon of confidence, the confidence of solitude. I watch the road in the rearview mirror as it unfurls behind me like a tormented tongue. I will leave this place and go back to the city. I will!

I drive, past the Old Place where I turned over the tobacco cart, *Don't dwell*, past the old stick barns that are slowly sinking into the ground because no one has use for them anymore and no one has the heart to finish them off, *Don't dwell*, past Baseline Road and the marker where Warrens is thinning trees for pulp, past the train trestle where Joe Brooks was lynched, yes, lynched! Not beheaded by some passenger train, but by locals, by my hometown ancestors, by people who looked like me and my family. Drive, I tell myself, don't dwell, drive, past the Indian trading path—or the place where it was thought to lie—that once stretched from Albany to Augusta, past the hunting camp, *Don't dwell*. Going away and coming back has altered my vision of it. It is a refractive error that distorts the landscape. My life as Southern autofiction. My life as Southern astigmatism.

It is impossible to think of the future here, because it is impossible to think of it changed. I pass the fire department and the ruritan club. On Lizard Slip Road, I see Palmer walking. He leans in my open window, glancing at the duffel bag in the passenger seat.

"You leaving?"

"I've got to go. I'm drowning here."

"It's dry as pith."

"I said it wrong. It's been so dry the trees will be bribing the dogs soon." I cringe, and wonder in alarm about this folksy Southernism, which I so carefully scrubbed from my speech long ago.

Palmer straightens, filling the window with his torso, shading me and shielding my eyes from the sun. His hands rest on the open window frame.

"Go ahead," he says gently. "Get some road spooled in you. You'll be back."

It's a curse. No! I want to shout, but I know he's right, so I say good-bye and roll up the window and drive. He remains in the middle of the road, and in the rearview mirror I see the dust swirl around him until he has disappeared into the dirt road's pale powder. An apology for dusting him seems called for, and yet if I turn back, I will have to drive away again, dusting him anew. We might go on in the endless loop of dusting and returning and dusting and so on without progress of any sort. I know he is there, walking the road in his worn-out shoes, walking the truth of all we refuse to acknowledge. He walks the length of this land, saying with each footfall, that's not why, that's not why, that's not why. He is a man, walking our town, day unto day, as his father walks, night unto night. I can't remember who said the South is the land of the mind. Or if that's even what they said. But for me it is simply land mine land mine landmine.

I HEAR THE old railroad tune as the tires take me away: *Southern serves the South. Southern gives the green light to in-no-va-tion.* The jingle I once loved makes me deeply uneasy, as does the sound of a train in the dark. Somewhere out there a man is looking for his head, because Christ is not the only one who haunts this land. As I pick up speed to flee once more, the tires take on an urgent tone, as they lap the road, repeating ceaselessly: *Don't dwell. Don't dwell. Don't dwell.*

I can't stay and I can't leave. I pull the car over and a dry, ragged sound escapes my throat. I drive back to the house in defeat. June doesn't wake from her nap until I park. As she scrambles out, something on the floor of the back seat catches my eye. It's a tiny stuffed animal, a dirty horse on a keychain like the ones children wear on backpacks. Lily. I have to return it, I think, just before I remember that Lily Langley is dead.

SOMEONE IS KNOCKING. It must be a stranger because the knocking is coming from the front door, which hasn't been opened in years. I yank it unstuck and stumble back as it swings open.

It's the warden, a tall man with a boyish face, pimples dotting his cheeks like inflamed freckles.

"Ma'am," he says, in the Southern way. "I'm Shep Shephard, with Fish and Wildlife. Did you call about a dead animal that looks like a wolf?"

He's young and ruddy and it's hard to tell whether he's embarrassed or amused.

"You got here fast."

"Some widow out at Blounts Creek called about a camp of bats in her attic. So I was out this way."

"I thought it was a colony of bats."

"Well, it wasn't any kind of bats after all. The bats were in her head. In her attic was a nest of yellowjackets, big as a basketball. I could have called the pest guys, but I was there so I sprayed it myself."

I tell him I hope he hasn't been stung.

"No, I watch and learn their flight path. Also, it's better if you're not nervous."

"Why?"

"If you're nervous, they will know. They will know and they will get you."

"I wouldn't have thought yellowjackets were covered by Fish and Wildlife."

His face is animated when he says, "People know I'm something of a body collector. The smaller the better."

"You collect insects?"

"There's a new institute up in Raleigh, a cryonics place. They're taking whole insects and small mammals."

"You mean cryonics as in freezing dead people in the hopes of bringing them back to life?"

"It's already worked on certain insects, including some grasshoppers I supplied. They need good specimens to experiment on. They've got a standing order for bats."

"The resurrection of grasshoppers."

Shep gives me a grave look. "It's legitimate science, you know. Cool something to liquid nitrogen temperature and decay stops. Don't you know anyone who's been revived after being technically dead? What's the difference except time?"

"This does seem like the right place to experiment with things suspended in time."

"It's called cryonic suspension. It's real," he says with annoyance. "Now, about this *wolf* you found."

"He's in the freezer."

"The freezer?" The pimply youth speaks to me as to a child.

"You're a fan of cryonics, right?" I say, and he laughs with a little puff.

"Is your husband home?" he says, and I realize he thought my joke was a barb.

"There's no husband. Follow me."

I lead him down the hall. "There's some dispute about

whether red wolves are hybrids or genetically distinct. What do you think?"

He shrugs and gives me the look I've seen many times from students, a look between indifference and dismissiveness, *Yeah, whatever lady.*

"Genetic ancestry gets tricky, doesn't it?"

"Look, I seriously doubt you've got a wolf. You're here all by yourself?"

"My family is dead."

He raises his eyebrows. "You said on the phone your last name is Ruskin? Is that the car crash on 64, where they waited for the jaws of life to come from Greenvale? The older couple that died—"

"My parents."

"And their son, Garland, who called the sheriff about donating his—"

"My brother."

"That's rotten luck. Really, what are the odds? Unless you're a witch," he says, in a not entirely joking tone. "Are you?"

"Are you a wolf in Shep's clothing?"

"Good one. Heard it before though."

"Not the first time I've been called a witch either."

We're standing at the door of the laundry room and suddenly I don't want to go in.

"It's too bad your brother didn't call the cryonics lab instead."

"He didn't want to come back."

"We're not taking humans yet anyway, but there's a place in Michigan that is. It's crazy expensive right now. But he could have saved his head at least."

"That's what he most wanted to be rid of."

He holds the door open for me, as though this is not my house.

"I found the wolf by the garden. He'd been eating a rabbit that was still in his mouth. I wasn't sure when you'd get here, that's why I put him in the freezer."

"You shouldn't have done that. I hope you used gloves."

"Yes."

I lift the lid of the freezer chest. There he is, sweet old wolf. The tarp has slipped around his neck and he looks sated and sleeping after eating Red's grandmother. *You know, my dear, it isn't safe for a little girl to walk through these woods alone.*

"This is one weird looking coyote," Shep says, taking a clothespin from the laundry line running across the room. He pokes at the pitiful wolf, all alone in his beautiful wolf body.

We look at the lumpen fur with its glassy, vacant eyes. "Is it a wolf or a coyote?"

"Hard to tell, isn't it? I'll take him in for testing. We'll find out exactly what it is, and maybe what killed it."

I move closer. "It looks like a coyote, but it's got a snout like a wolf."

"They're interbreeding. We call them coywolves. They're predators who have no predators."

"What if someone's killing them off?"

"Seems unlikely. Most people here shoot what they kill. I don't see any gunshot wounds," he says, taking the tarp off the defenseless mammal.

"None visible. What if it is a red wolf?"

"The penalty for killing a wolf is a year in prison and

$100,000 fine. But we don't know that this is a wolf or that anyone killed it. You said you found it in the garden?"

I nod and debate telling him about the first wolf, the one I buried by the old barn. I should probably keep my mouth shut.

"Death sure does find you lady."

"You're wondering whether I'm a wolf killer? No. Not a coyote killer either."

He squints at me, and lowers the freezer lid. "All right. We'll test for poison, for rabies, and send for DNA results."

He goes out to his truck for gloves and a plastic shroud. I offer to help, but he shoos me away, and loads the wolf by himself.

"Try not to find any more dead bodies, but if you do, call me. Don't touch them or move them or freeze them. Call and let me handle it."

THIRTEEN

THE FUNERAL IS on Sunday, and the church parking lot is nearly full. Tobias was right; the whole town is here.

Inside, on this warm and sunny September afternoon, I see a dead body for the second time. I was not here to identify Garland or my parents, and though I've been to other funerals, for those the body was ash.

Lily is at the front of the church, below the pulpit, before the communion table: *This Do in Remembrance of Me*. She has been rouged and arranged and dressed in a high-necked white taffeta gown. The frill around her throat covers the wound. It is the sort of dress young girls here often wear for weddings, so that they look like child brides as they skip up the church aisle scattering petals. Lily is no one's bride and never will be. Lily is five. She was five. She will never again be a girl running through the summer dark, catching fireflies and twirling with the freedom only children know, spinning above the spinning earth. We are here to put her in the ground.

Tobias takes my elbow and guides me to a seat. The church has changed little over my lifetime, though the hard wood pews are padded now and the windows' original wavy glass has been replaced with thicker amber-hued panes. The ceiling is high; the walls unadorned except for a wooden cross and a board with numbers that slide into slots recording the previous week's attendance and collection: 51, $283.27.

Looking at that board with its modest numbers makes me tremble to think that I could be at JFK staring at a different board, digital and seemingly infinite, with departures to anywhere in the world I wished to go.

Minister Swain takes his place at the podium above Lily and gathers his notes tremulously. "This is beyond our human understanding, but our Lily has been called home."

The woman two pews ahead buries her face in her hands, and I realize it is Lily's mother. A man beside her, who must be the father, Burl, tightens his grip on her shoulder. Between them, just above the high-back pew, I see the top of Tom's head, a spike of red hair sticking up like a bare stalk.

"I know it's hard, friends," Minister Swain says, "but today Lily is with the Lord in Paradise. God is not going to lead us out of our grief. He is going to lead us through it."

I sit on my hands, which shake with anger at this senseless death, and fury at myself for turning her away.

"I ask that we sing Lily home, with 'In the Sweet By and By,' the first and last verses, standing on the last." The country voices begin the song I've known since I've known words, and I listen without a lip movement, as the faithful sing around me.

There's a land that is fairer than day,
And by faith we can see it afar,

For the father waits over the way,
To prepare us a dwelling place there.
In the sweet by and by,
We shall meet on that beautiful shore

Minister Swain lifts his hands and we rise.

We shall meet, we shall sing, we shall reign,
In the land where the saved never die

"Friends, today we come to bury Lily and to praise God through our grief. The Lord gave, the Lord hath taken away, blessed be the name of the Lord."

"Amen."

My hands start to twitch under my thighs. My legs shake.

"We pray for this suffering family, that God's grace may surround them, and that in this hour of grief and trial, they may feel the presence and succor of Him, who tells us to lay our burdens down in his presence."

Lily's face, the image of her clear and curious eyes, has found its way inside, just as Professor's did, with his buzzcut and his way of squinching his face to hold on to his glasses. It's in my marrow, in the muck where my heart was.

"Young Lily, whose death we mourn, was a joyous and spirited child of endless energy and, if I may say, relentless questions."

A soft laugh wafts up the aisle at these last words, offering encouragement and punctuation from the flock.

"Lily endeared herself to all, from her family to her classmates to all of us who knew her. She was a delightful and affectionate child, kind, and lively, and it is easy to see how she embedded herself in our hearts. That will not change. We will carry her there."

I hate this church.

"Sometimes, friends, life is a fiery trial. In these difficult days let us remember that Lily has gone to Him who said: 'Suffer the little children to come unto me, and forbid them not, for of such is the kingdom of heaven.' Blessed be God."

"Blessed be God."

I lean forward, clutching the pew ahead. I open my mouth and Tobias puts his hand on my back.

"Tilly and Burl and young Tom, we are here as a family to pray with you and offer our sturdy shoulders and open hearts as you grieve the loss of Lily. The death of a child is an event that can test our faith, but it is also an opportunity to recognize God's sovereignty. It is easy to ask why God let Lily live for only five years. Friends, God didn't make Lily live for five years. God makes Lily live for eternity."

I STEADY MYSELF as we file out of the church, pausing to shake hands with Tilly, Burl, and Tom, stricken and silent in the vestibule by the door. It's hardly a time to introduce myself to his parents, so I grasp hands with each of them, pausing to hug Tom, and step outside into the obscene sun.

I walk past the milling funeral-goers, and turn toward home.

"Rachel, wait. I'll drive you to the burial," Tobias says.

"I'm not going."

"The hardest part is over. Don't you want to see it through?"

"Do I want to see a five-year-old put in the ground? I do not." My voice breaks, and I feel my head shaking like a wobble doll on my stiff neck. And maybe I'm made of the same stuff, a lot of nothing inside, and I want him to pick me up and carry me off and lay me down and cover me with a quilt. But why should I be comforted? Why should either of us be allowed comfort in each other?

"At least let me drive you then." He is about to cry and I can't bear it. I don't want to see anyone's tears or hear the useless religious words.

"I want to walk," I say, roughly, twisting away from him as he reaches for my hand. I want to be alone.

IN THE EVENING, June and I try to settle on the couch to watch the summer dim of September twilight. But I'm too tormented. The train whistles as it passes this stopless place, and the coyotes respond, eerie and loud, with yips and howls. A leader starts them off, barking sharply, and the others chime in for the pastoral evensong. I turn on a documentary on the photographer Sally Mann, almost out of desperation. Maybe she can sort this. She's explaining how, unlike Proust, she's looking for flaws, the angel of *un*certainty, on her glass negatives, when the noise sounds above. June lets out a snore. But Sally Mann's beautiful romanticism can't help me now. I run up the attic stairs, and begin tumbling through stacks of my family's history. Garland's baseball cleats, his FFA trophy, his butter-soft baseball glove. He didn't want anything of his old life. I yank them from their pile and drop them to the floor. Registering in an instant the memory of Garland with each item, I fling one after another, first to the floor and then farther away, down the attic stairs. June races in, assisting enthusiastically by taking things in her teeth, as I try to dismantle my family history in objects. I pick up a rope coiled on top of a box. June, thinking it is a game, begins to tug it away.

I drop the rope, sending her skittering. I hurl things down the stairs, as she watches, confused. I see the photo of me and Garland under the rifle rack and I snatch it up and start to tear it. June gives me a look as though she's the sober nurse on standby with the meds and, I almost shout, I *am* the madwoman in the attic, as I rip the picture in two. But I have second thoughts and shove it in my pocket.

"What am I doing, June? I don't know!" Suddenly, I do. "We're going to have a bonfire."

At the edge of the lawn, just before the garden, I pile my family's belongings, and light the fire. At first, it is a slow burn, but within ten minutes, it threatens to spread beyond my control. I stand holding the garden hose, watching my family's ghosts gyre up in smoke. As the flames leap, I put my finger on the nozzle to increase the pressure. The fire smokes and protests, but I contain the flames, alternating between burning and hosing my history.

Beside me, June begins to growl, the fur rising along her back.

"What is it?"

She's looking toward the woods, and I lift my eyes and see him. The wolf is watching. He is looking into my eyes, into my soul, into my life. *He knows.* My heart hurts; my tongue is dry. I shush June, but the sound comes out thick and strained. She barks three times, but the barks are fearful.

I kneel before the fire, watching him against the dark trees, mysterious and exposed to everything this Southern sky has brought down.

I want to burn farm and field, every single thing I come from. The tobacco taunts from the other side of the drive. Even here, crouching by the fire, looking away from the field, I can smell it, and see in memory the beauty of the deep deep green. Our entire lives lived wrong, and no one to tell us. If they had, it wouldn't have mattered. We would not have believed them, but we were soiled all the same.

June whimpers, but does not leave my side.

"Go to the house."

She won't. The fire smokes and hisses. I run the hose until it dies down. The wolf watches without a movement.

HOURS LATER, we are back inside with Sally Mann when Tobias knocks on the door, to June's joy.

"I saw smoke and was worried."

"You were watching the house?"

"I was sitting outside, couldn't sleep. Doesn't that ever happen to you?"

"Yes. That's why I was burning the things that keep me up at night."

"Good luck with that."

I try to send him away, but he's stubborn and I'm weak. It's been a hard day of dredged memories, and the surrounding dark is unsettling. We sit in lawn chairs, watching the low orange of the last embers.

"Rachel, I'm worried about Tom. He's sensitive, he's *good*. He reminds me of Garland."

"Why are you telling me?"

"Because you know better than any of us what he's going through. You and Garland, the shooting—"

"Why is it still happening? Because nothing is ever done about it. Because no one is ever responsible."

"His grandmother gave him the gun. Should she be in jail?"

"They wouldn't charge the grandmother. They'd charge the parents with failing to properly store a firearm."

"That's better? Rip the family apart and put the grieving parents in jail?"

"It's a fine, there won't be jail time. Nothing is going to change until adults are charged."

"You were involved in a shooting death years ago. Do you wish your own father had been charged?"

"Yes."

"I don't believe you."

"Tobias, I don't care whether you believe me. If this is my view, I can't expect my family to be spared. That's the problem. Everyone thinks their own personal belief is all that matters. I don't care what you believe. I care about justice."

"We care about tradition here. We care about history."

"The South doesn't have history! The South has myth."

"It has both," he retorts, taking me by surprise. "And what do you mean by that anyway?"

I blush, realizing that now that I'm being questioned on one of my clever summations of the South, I'm not quite sure what to say. "That instead of acknowledging our history, instead of using that rich religious language we're so full of, we never atoned or even repented. We create myths so we can forget the past."

"People don't like to be reminded," he says. "That doesn't mean they don't remember."

I realize I've spoken rashly, stupidly, and I hate to feel stupid here, although I always do. I can never reconcile the shame I feel about this place with the love I felt for it as a child. Feel, felt, should feel, have felt. Stick to one tense, my favorite English teacher wrote on a high school paper, shifting tenses makes you seem uncertain and irresolute.

"I don't want to argue, Rachel. I want to talk about Tom. He's going to need us."

But instead of talking we tense into silence, staring at the smoky pile in the center of the yard, like the dark eye of a gruesome single-eyed monster.

"Rachel," he says finally, "do you remember your dad's dog, Blue?"

"The feisty one whose ear was torn by a raccoon."

"Right, a good dog. A little fearful maybe, a little hesitant at first, but he was a good dog. You know when the raccoon tore his ear, Blue was swimming across the canal, and she was sitting on his head, trying to hold him under so he'd drown."

I notice his slide from the genderless "raccoon" to "she."

"Why are you telling me this?"

I knew a raccoon bit Blue's ear. Dad and Garland sewed it closed with fishing twine. At the time I thought they were too cheap to pay the vet to stitch it up. But later another dog's ear was split, and they took her to the vet, and the ear got infected.

"That's only part of it. Everybody knows your dad was gifted at training animals. He turned Blue into a good dog, so good there was a lot of interest in him. Your dad sold him to a man in Vanceboro, who took him on bear hunts."

"How do you know?"

"Because we saw them later at regionals. The man brought Blue over, and told us a bear had attacked him. 'He hasn't been the same since,' the man told us. And your dad said, 'That's not Blue.' But it was, the man swore it was. He had scars from the attack, but his face was different. 'He is so changed,' your dad said. 'So *changed*.'"

"Tobias, what are you trying to say?"

"I'm saying some things are not meant to change. Now don't jump on me. I'm not saying anything about the South or its history. I'm talking about people, individuals. How when we change, it's not always for the better. First, Blue was punished by the raccoon, a fair punishment meted out in self defense, and Blue accepted that. Then a bear attacked him, and he couldn't recover."

"No one changes here. If you want change, you leave."

"Don't be bitter, Rachel," he says, putting his warm hand on my arm and looking at the smoldering ashes wafting white drops in the leaden air. "I'm only saying that we each act according to our natures. There's nothing wrong with that in itself."

"Thanks for the country philosophy."

"You always were too smart for us. But it's the people here who'd do anything for you. We'd pull you out of fire."

"Yes, but you'd be the ones who started it in the first place!"

June has been napping in the house, and she pushes at the screen door with her nose.

"You don't care about tradition, do you, June?" I ask, opening the door. "You don't care about history."

June licks his hand and leans in for a scratch.

"Dogs like a man around."

"Oh, please."

"I'm teasing, Rachel. We're all animals though, whether on two legs or four."

"Finally something we can agree on."

Looking toward the woods, I think of the wolf. *So here I find you, you old sinner*, the hunter says in the story. *I've been hunting you for a long time.*

"Did you leave someone behind in New York?"

"That's none of your business."

"Just trying to assess."

"Assess what?"

"Whether you're here to hide or to live."

"You're going to tell me about living?"

"Isn't there comfort in being where you're known? I've known you and your family your whole life. Saw you grow up. Saw you itching to leave. And here you are."

"You told me a story about Blue. Now let me tell you a story about a different blue."

"Fair enough."

"I had to see a cardiologist last year in New York."

"Nothing serious, I hope."

"I fainted; it turned out to be nothing. It's the flight response. I have a sensitive vagal nerve. In the office after the exam, the surprisingly chatty doctor—he thought I was a writer—told me he was haunted by a story that he had tried to write about himself, but he couldn't find a form. It was something he had heard on the radio, about an experiment in which mice were trained to be terrified of blue lights.

"I'm sure they tortured them and did horrible things to get this result, he told me. But generations later, mice that had never before been exposed exhibited fear on seeing blue lights."

"You know," Tobias says, "I read that deer born on the East Side of Berlin after the wall came down would still not cross to the West Side even though the wall was gone."

Instead of asking him the source of this gem, I say, "You agree suffering can be inherited?"

"Sure, we've all got a package on our backs. That's what my grandmother used to say."

"Some have heavier packages to bear."

"Yes, that's in the nature of things."

He gives me the old slyly seductive look, and I feel the invisible cord of attraction we've always had tighten and tug. I'm tempted to let Tobias spend the night, to have someone to reach for when the coyotes howl, but I want to grieve alone.

"You have this way," he says, leaning toward me, "of putting your hand around your throat. Are you trying to protect yourself or choke yourself?"

I self-consciously lower my hand and hold it awkwardly in my lap, unsettled that my body is disobeying me with a nervous habit I thought I'd broken. I thought I had solved the Tobias problem, too—no local love to hold me back—but he disarms me still. He moves closer and places a warm hand on my knee. I'm confused with desire that I thought had died with youth, desire so strong it charged the air. Settle yourself, I say silently. You are a woman of middle age, not a schoolgirl.

"That won't help anything," I say, moving away.

It's his turn to blush, and I notice his tiredness, which only emphasizes his good looks, his expectant eyes. "Don't be like that."

"This is exactly how I am."

He leaves without speaking, standing and moving slowly as though injured, and I sit in the dark remembering nights like this, nights with Tobias, but other nights, too, of childhood and fireflies and the night I killed the best friend I've ever had. June nudges me and licks my hand, and then, my feet, as though anointing me.

IT'S HOT AND I can't sleep. In the shower I find dirt under my nails and a thin ring around my neck, and I am filled with the old fear of being dirty. The soil is in us. I scrub my nails until my cuticles bleed, and dirt lodges in the cuts. I dig it out with Garland's pocketknife.

Professor was also haunted by dirt. We used to tease him that he'd been "cured" like the tobacco after the time when he was eight that he was briefly locked in the barn after the gas burners were turned on. The leaves had been primed and looped and tied on the sticks that were hung from the barn beams, all five hundred of them. We were standing around the cooler drinking cold soda when someone finally asked, where's Professor? They cut the gas and opened the barn, and we were all slightly surprised that after a few days he was fine. People looked for things to be wrong with him. It was spoken of as an accident, but we all knew whose hand slid the stick locking the door latch—everybody knew. The lead bully was a boy named Vick, but his father owned the lumber mill and was the richest man around, so no one said anything.

I sat beside Professor on the grass while he recovered. His shorn hair was wet with sweat and his face glistened like Gabriel.

"It's always dark," he said finally.

"What's dark?"

"Inside the barn. It's always dark, and the floor is always cool, even in summer. The leaves were hanging over my head."

"What are you talking about, P? Does your brain hurt?"

"When the door was locked. The wet leaves were hanging above me, dripping on my head and arms, legs, too."

"What dripped on you?"

"From the leaves. It's sticky. It sticks to your skin."

"Tobacco leaves are sticky," I said, and patted his head, and thought, the best boy in the world has gone sick in the head.

"At night the dirt rings round the drain like the inside of a tree trunk."

"Professor," I said, "you're talking kind of crazy."

"Don't you care, Rachel?"

"I care. I just can't feature what you're saying."

"You have to scrub yourself hard. When the barn's been put in. When the leaves are hanging from the sticks in rows. You know how they do it?"

"Do what?"

"Cure it. They break it off the stalk. They hang it; they lock it up and turn the burners on. You kill the web first, then the stem. It takes six days."

"What does?"

"To kill it out. When you can pop the stalk, when it bends between your fingers, then the stem is dead and the curing is over."

"Professor, you just sit here. Catch your breath and I'll take you home to get cleaned up."

"Why are we always dirty?"

"We just have to scrub."

"This sticky stuff won't come off."

"Yes, it will. You just have to use the special soap. I'll give you some."

FOURTEEN

I LOOK AT the golden field while I sip coffee and listen to the radio. But the news feels too far away. Or I feel too far away. The world I need to pay attention to is just outside. My father was right. You can't live everywhere.

The scent of smoldering ashes is in the air, and I am alarmed in the caffeinated daylight at my nighttime arson. I had witnessed from a distance the controlled burning of undergrowth in the woods surrounding the farm. But I had never in my life started a fire.

June and I set off, and I see how walking is Palmer's answer: Slough it off in steps. Palmer's walking reinforces the town's memory. As for me, I want to forget. I want to forget that I bossed Professor, and then, I killed him. It was an accident, but I have lived in terror that the seeds of violence are still inside me. Once they broke through, and I live very carefully so that they stay dormant and don't germinate.

Half a mile in, Palmer appears in the distance; no one

else has his pace or posture. We catch up and fall in step beside him.

"Back already?" he says.

"I never even left."

"Happens to the best of us," he says. "I wish my father had left when he had a chance, but he wanted to buy a piece of land."

I'm afraid to ask what land, but I am seized by the need to know. The story about Four Corners is that my great grandfather, through grit and stubbornness and more than a little chicanery, acquired the plots. But the chicanery was kept vague, and the only thing I heard was about a good horse and a bad card game.

"Was it Four Corners he wanted?"

The four fields my great grandfather bought one at a time and brought together into a hundred-acre farm that made more money than most because of the large tobacco allotment. The four fields that grew what I had often heard called the best tobacco in the county. The four fields that sent me to college. The four fields that helped me escape.

"Maybe so, maybe not. Even if it was, they wouldn't have sold it to him anyway. The land's too good."

Fields surround us, stick barns in prolonged states of collapse. When I was ten, we changed from stick to bulk barns. The long truck came up the dusty road, small in the heat-shimmered distance, then closer, larger, still shimmering. The truck unloaded the shiny metal trailers noisily, making the quiet after seem new and changed. Now the bulk barns are old, too, rusting and weatherworn.

"Where are you off to?" Palmer asks, changing the subject, and I worry that I've overstepped, and asked too many questions. But when I say this, he stops walking to respond.

"Don't worry about questions. Don't worry about talking. It's the not talking that's the problem. We should all be talking all the time. I'm eighty-five years old, and I have made myself available. Not because I want to be, but because I have to be. This is what I have to do."

June recognizes our turnoff and barks eagerly, dancing in the dirt road. I gesture across the ditch. "I've been going to the Red Dredge in the afternoons, to sit in Garland's old deer stand."

Palmer nods and continues on his route as June and I enter the woods. The path is hard to find, and for a while we just walk, June and I, brushing against briars. Red scratches appear on my hands, a creeper catches my shirt, then another, and it takes minutes to break out of the thicket.

The patch of beech trees appears before us, Beech Island, not nearly as far as it had seemed when I was a child. We pick up the pace as we approach the swimming hole, the Red Dredge. It's not as wide as it seemed then, but it probably still creates a current after a big rain. Everyone here knows why it's called the Red Dredge. How years and years ago some Northerners came to section off areas of the Little Dismal. How they cut a canal with a red walking dredge but the Depression came, the company went broke, and "that was that." The wood dredge rotted away years ago, but locals never change a name, even when the thing itself is gone.

It's deserted. First, it was forbidden to girls—it was for skinny-dipping boys only—and now it is forbidden to everyone. It seems today's children obey this. Maybe they think it is haunted. Maybe they prefer a different sort of danger, and the Dredge does not excite their imaginations the way it did ours.

At the water, I drop to my knees. My reflection disappears as I blow on the surface, then returns and disappears again as

June noses in, lapping and dripping. She crashes ahead joyfully, and I follow her, fully clothed as for baptismal. Dark trees surround us, and the sky is a gray circle above the ring of pines. Places have language, and this was my first. Maybe that's why I was cast out of the academy. I never acquired the tongue for it.

This is where Garland taught me the backstroke, the breaststroke, the dead man's float. Professor watched timidly from knee-deep water, as Garland showed me how to lie face down and breathe out slowly, as my hair fanned out around my head like a jellyfish. Careful, he said, slow, and my body started to sink. When I was tired of being dead, he held me afloat, saying how light I was in the water. How long can you hold me, Garland? Till the cows come home. How long is that? Till kingdom come. Then we heard the train whistle and we waded back to Professor and the three of us talked about all the places we would travel—Rocky Mount, Richmond, Fredericksburg, Alexandria, Washington, DC!

The drop-off takes me by surprise, but I don't resist and instead dive down, remembering how, as children, we tried to reach the bottom of the world "or maybe China." June paddles around, barking; her bay pleasantly muffled under water. It surprises me when I lift my head and find I have broken the surface. My body is refusing to sink. I dive again, remembering my brother's instructions. Let your body go limp. Don't breathe, don't breathe, don't breathe. I sink through the water, through the years, see my mother's sweet face, then my father's, Garland's, and deeper still, Professor, with his cowlick and his chubby cheeks. I might be able to sink deep enough to find the part of me that lives here on the bottom, submerged in the dark chill.

"I don't want to," Garland whispered all those years ago. He was just a boy. So was Professor. We were just kids with guns.

I don't realize I'm in danger until my body begins to fight, swimming up, up, pushing water with my hands and grasping for something solid. *Don't panic* are the first words to return. June is paddling, frantically, in circles, barking. I cough and she comes over, nudging me, half pushing me toward the shore. The first time I reach down with my foot I don't find the bottom, but the Dredge is not the sea and the second time I touch sand. I drag myself out of the water and crawl onto the bank.

Kneeling on all fours, I bow my head, press my palms into the ground, and wait. Is this the face of a witch, I ask my reflection in the water? No answer comes, no lightning, no tears. I stand and brush dirt from my knees.

It is like an apparition. A raccoon has found a crab apple and taken it to the water to wash. He sits at the edge, chewing quickly and turning the fruit in his efficient little hands. Something is amiss. He's acting strange and doesn't run off as June bounds toward him. She's a failed hunter, but the impulse remains. As a child, I had been to one shocking family day at the hunting club. The big event was to pull a caged raccoon across the water while the dogs swam after it in a frenzy. The raccoon clawed at the cage in terror, trying to get free. June cannot help it. She is being pulled by the line herself. She lunges at the raccoon and the masked animal pounces.

"June!"

If an animal doesn't fear you, don't go near it.

"Go!" I throw a rock, but they are entangled and it misses both of them. Holding a branch like a spear, I approach the bodies that are in a fight for life. I strike at the raccoon, aiming for the head. *Aim for the heart*, my father told us during target practice, but a stick is not a gun. I strike again and again. The raccoon grabs the stick and lunges at me as June jumps between us. I have time to kick the raccoon hard in the belly, with a sickening feeling as my foot connects with the soft organs under his fur. He hisses, and wobbles like a drunk, then scurries under a bush.

June has a bloody nose and she sinks into my arms. "Come on," I coax, leading her through the woods. She makes it halfway home, and I carry her the rest. As soon as I see the driveway, I break into a run, joggling June in my arms. I dump her on the front seat of the car and take off for town. I don't know what to do, where to go. The vet is twenty miles away. As I pass the p.o., I see Tobias standing by his truck, talking. He waves, and in one moment I curse him and this small-town nosiness, and simultaneously realize he'll know what to do. I skid into the gravel lot and jump out of the car.

"What's your hurry, New York?"

"June's been bitten by a rabid raccoon."

Without a word, he gets in his truck and motions for me to follow. At his house, he works quickly and efficiently, cleaning June's wounds. He sends me home to get her papers. When I return, he has already given her a booster, assuming that my father would have seen to her shots. He calls the health department while I sit on his kitchen floor, cradling June in my arms. She whimpers and snuggles like a baby. I infuriate myself by crying. Tobias squeezes my shoulder, but I shrug him off. June and I embrace on the floor for a long time. Finally, she dozes, snoring softly, and I stand on weakened legs.

Tobias asks where we encountered the raccoon, and leaves with his gun. I spend two hours doing nothing, making tea, sitting at the table. Once I open the door to go outside, and June stirs, cutting her eyes at me in accusation.

When Tobias returns, and nods to tell me the killing is done, I take his hand. Upstairs in his room, we undress in silence. I turn away to adjust the blind blowing in the breeze, and he turns me to face him.

"Remember me?" he says, serious and unsmiling.

My skin is hot and prickly as we ease onto the bed. With his solid body and coarse hands, he gives me first the absorption then the incognizance I want. It is bliss to feel without thinking, to touch without talking.

"Are you all right?" he asks as I dress.

"I don't know."

IN THE KITCHEN, June is stirring. Tobias carries her to the car, and we drive her to the vet, where she has to be quarantined. The vet, an older man with a prophet's beard, warns that if she shows any symptoms of rabies she'll have to be euthanized.

ALONE IN THE Juneless hush of the house, I watch over the farm and fields as the sun sets. The blue pales, then the sky applies her rouge in wild streaks before the looming moon.

I miss June. I even miss the one upstairs, who has gone quiet as suddenly and mysteriously as it announced itself. I wasn't going to chase you away, I want to tell the ghost. I was going to learn to live with you. In the empty attic, I lie on the floor and try to slip my skin. There is no husband to rub red pepper in my flesh. I could easily return at dawn, unmissed and unnoticed.

FIFTEEN

SHEP THE GAME warden is back. "You again!" he says, with playful suspicion. I corroborate Tobias's story. He has already turned over the raccoon's remains for testing, though it seems certain it's a case of rabies. Shep tells me to call if I see any animals behaving strangely.

"And the wolf?"

"You're in the clear. It wasn't a wolf; it was a hybrid, a coywolf, just as I suspected. His brains have tested negative for rabies. It's distemper that killed him."

"Distemper? I have that myself."

"It's a virus," he says sternly, "not"—he gestures with his hand—"a mood. Not for the coywolves anyway. I don't know what kind you have."

I ignore his scolding, or maybe he's stating a fact. I don't know what kind I have either.

"Are you sure it wasn't a wolf? It *looked* like a wolf."

"Looks deceive."

Something thumps above our heads. It's the attic. Something is dropping. Something is falling. Something is here.

"What's that?" he says, looking at the ceiling.

"My ghost," I say, with as neutral an expression as I can muster.

"In the attic?"

I nod.

"Lady, I think you've got bats."

After trips to his truck and up to the attic, he finds the culprit. It's one lonely bat, taken away unceremoniously in a garbage bag. Apparently, he had been trapped up there for a while and was thumping out his final days, unseen and misunderstood. How did I not think of the obvious, I ask myself. Of course it was a bat!

ALONE AGAIN, the house is oppressively silent. The quiet that I had enjoyed so much is ruined. I miss June. I miss Lyric. I miss my ghost who turned out to be a bat. I attack the garden. Don't dwell, I tell myself, as I yank weeds. Tobias arrives with Tom. It's our first meeting since what the church calls acts of the flesh, and it makes him almost shy. I'm clammy and quivery with embarrassment and desire. It's all too much and not enough, so I look at them through what I hope is an expressionless, indifferent mask.

"I was just coming to check," Tobias says.

"On?"

"You. Are you all right?"

"Yes," I say, pausing to toss a vine on the pile of discards.

"What are you doing?" Tom asks.

"I'm clearing the garden so I can plant for fall."

"Do you need some help?" Tobias asks, a little too quickly.

"No."

"Weren't you doing that the first time we came?" Tom asks.

"I'm a slow learner."

Tobias and Tom stand side by side, united in skepticism, surveying my work.

"There are better methods," Tobias says. "How are you going to prepare the soil?"

"I'm going to fluff it with a fork." I back away, trying to gain some distance from Tobias, and he wisely shifts subjects.

"Tom is working with me this week. I'm showing him the ways of tobacco farming."

"Is that what you're doing, Tom?"

"I guess."

I look at Tobias over the boy's head, and he gazes back, evenly. A memory flashes of him on the bed's edge, hurriedly taking off his boots in movements boyish and endearing.

"We're finishing up your field this week. It's the last one. Then Tom and I are going to the auction. Aren't we Tom?"

Tom nods. I feel for this child who will have to live through adulthood haunted by a childhood crime. The guilt will never go away, but I'm angry with Tobias for bringing him here. It's an invasion of privacy, a useless gesture of good intention.

"There's a meeting at the church tonight," Tobias says. "Tom's parents might be charged, and there's a town meeting to discuss a possible protest."

"They won't be charged."

"You don't know that," he says, not rising to the bait.

"They won't be charged," I repeat, glancing at Tom and trying to soften the edge in my voice. "No one ever is."

Tom moves away from us, stiff faced and shuffling his feet.

"A church meeting about guns?" I say, letting the anger into my voice now that Tom is out of earshot.

"It's the only building big enough."

"They could have it in a barn."

He looks at me, and I remember keeping him waiting behind a barn twenty-five years ago, a sunburned man with shaggy hair and thoughtful eyes who would leave blueberries on the back steps because he would not come in the house when he was dirty from the field. He is a handsome man.

"Will armed doormen be there?"

"Rachel, if you want to come, you'll be heard. You can also listen."

Tobias has work to do, and he wants to leave Tom with me. I can't say no, with him standing there in his freckles and untied shoes.

"DID YOUR BROTHER shoot someone, too?" Tom asks, when we're alone, drinking lemonade on the grass.

"No, I did. I was your age when I shot my best friend, Rufus."

"Did you think the gun was unloaded?" he asks, after a pause.

"I thought Rufus was a deer."

"Oh," he says, as though this makes sense. In fact, this child knows better than anyone I've ever met. "I wish I was a deer."

I freeze, afraid of what he might be saying in the shadow of his sister's death. But I have to know.

"Why a deer, Tom?"

"Because they don't have to talk to anybody. They get to run free in the woods."

I don't say, they're often hunted and killed. What do I know of what it's like to be a deer, *really*. It seems likely that fear is inherited, the bequeathal of prey to prey. But maybe they do run free and only respond to the chase with instinct. Maybe they have no sense of any time but now, this moment. Maybe their lives are lived outside the shape of our sad and terrible words: history, suffering, shame, *again*.

Tom is restless, and we circle the garden, inspecting the remains. I ask him what I should plant.

"I'm a beginner, remember. Also, we have to choose things that grow in the winter."

"What grows then?"

"Collards, cabbage, turnips."

"Yuck."

As we stand side by side looking at the weedy plot, I tell him about the secret room.

"Tom, I can't tell you what to do. Maybe this will sound silly. But when I was your age, I built myself a house."

"Where is it?"

"In my head."

"You built a house in your head?"

"Yes. I had all the rooms just like I wanted. There was one room way upstairs that I kept locked."

"Why?"

"Because I wasn't ready to look at what was inside."

"Did you lose the key?"

"No, that's the best part of this house. It has everything, and you can walk through it whenever you like. It had all my favorite things, my favorite people. But there was something I kept locked in a room."

"Was it a monster?"

"Sort of. It was a memory monster. I knew it was there and that I could face it when I was ready."

He turns his body in a full circle, scanning the yard, the field.

"I can't keep it in my head," he says. "It's in my whole body." He pinches his arm until it makes me so uncomfortable, I pull his hand away.

"It's in there," he says, plucking at his arms and neck, "under my skin."

"What is?"

"I don't know, but it's in me."

He and Lily were just outside their house, playing cops and robbers. He was simply stopping an escaped convict in the form of a pigtailed kindergartner, with what he thought was an unloaded gun.

"I know I'm too old for that pretend stuff," he says, and hits himself in the head with his fist. "Lily wanted to."

There's nothing I can say, so I tell him about June and how much I miss her, until he smiles faintly.

"You need a horse," he says, and plops down in the grass.

"I don't think so."

"Is it true what that lady says about you at the post office?" he asks.

"What does she say?"

"You think your poop doesn't stink."

It's funny, but it still smarts. I want to tell Tom you can't care too much or you'll be caught here forever. But what does it matter where you are, if you're lost to yourself?

"Do you know what that means?"

"You smell good?" he asks innocently.

"Everybody stinks some time, Tom."

SIXTEEN

MINISTER SWAIN IS at the door, greeting congregants, as though it's a church service and we're here for his sermon on the right to bear arms.

Tobias squeezes my elbow as we walk up the aisle to our seats, and I feel the eyes of the town on us. I'm of interest because they value certitude in all things and there are two unknowns—the state of my soul and my designs on one of their men.

My family's pew is fifth from last, on the left of the pulpit. We are early. My parents hated lateness more than anything. ("The sooner we get there, the sooner we can get home.") Compulsive punctuality is my inheritance. I have learned to enjoy it as it allows me to view people arriving.

Eva, the postmistress, and her alcoholic husband settle themselves a few pews ahead. As Eva turns her profile toward the window, the light on her parched skin is arresting. Her husband's drinking has taken a toll on his face, but it has taken a bigger toll on hers. While her husband drinks himself to death, her skin is slowly dying of thirst.

The churchgoers appear as plane passengers loading for the final ascent. First, Ms. Gertrude, impeccably dressed in her purple knit set and patting her blue hair as she walks down the aisle, thin and spry. She must be in her nineties now, stopping to speak to everyone. She's one of the passengers who need extra time for boarding. There are a few others with their canes and walkers, the gold club, arriving early to claim their spots. There is a seconds-long break, and then come the frequent flyers and the sky club members. Next the few families with young children, the Boyds and the Cutlers with their energetic offspring piling in the pews to smiles and nods. The economy folks, who might have decided to come at the last minute and will have to take the seats they can get. At least there's legroom—no prayer kneelers in this country church.

Dennis and Ernest from the bar are here. Ernest is clinging to the end of the pew for support or as a springboard to escape. Tom emerges from the choir room, mysteriously and alone, and goes to sit between his haggard parents.

Much of the town is here, but only the white farming families. Greenvale is slowly integrating, but, paradoxically, the church is the last space to open. And here in Shiloh, it's even slower. There's a missionary Baptist church founded in the 1890s by former slaves, and a more recent black church past Spivey's Crossroads. For townspeople, Shiloh Church of Christ has always been woven into a pattern of righteousness, but for others, it's a pattern of their, of our—I am from here and a part of this—of the South's, disgrace. Dr. King's quip is still true, that the most segregated hour in America is eleven o'clock on Sunday morning.

When everyone has settled in their pews and gone mute, looking to the pulpit as though we are children waiting for story hour, the three little pigs come in, proud and single file. From somewhere the phrase comes to me, the hunter in the lead should have the gun pointed ahead. Although hunters are supposed to walk abreast when possible, in sight of one another, for safety.

Vasta is first, the leader and the lookout, then the middle one, Pearl, the name rises from memory, and Annie, who is smiling and has flowers in her long hair tamed into plaits.

"Welcome," Minister Swain says, looking both pleased and conflicted that his church is so full, but not for his Sunday sermon.

"I'm going to turn this over to Andy Sawyer in a minute. But while I have all of you here, let's go through the prayer list."

A fifteen-minute medical report follows, detailing the suffering of the old and dying and the not so old and dying. There are Shilohans with cancer of the liver, the throat, the lung, and "the female kind." Someone has been hit by a truck; four others have faulty hearts. A conversation ensues about a woman who died of a mysterious attack on her daily early morning walk in a remote area. Dogs were found near her body, which was lying in a ditch. The dogs were tested for a DNA match, but, as Minister Swain reads from the sheriff's report, they were "unable to make a definitive determination" about what exactly attacked and killed Linda Alligood.

Earl Boyd blames a wolf. "Maybe the sheriff's office and NC Wildlife Commission can tell us another fairy tale as good as 'Unknown canine claws woman to death.' Odds are it was a wolf. For whatever reason, the government and the wildlife people are lying about the dangers of these animals."

"Friends," Minister Swain says, trying to regain control and turn from imagined villains to imagined saviors. "Let's pray for the families. We'll continue this discussion Sunday with an updated prayer list. Today we're here to talk about guns. As you know, after the events in Texas and South Carolina and elsewhere, Brothers Calvin and Graham have offered to guard the church doors during service. They are here today."

Everyone turns toward the church doors, and the two men lift their hands to their holsters.

Several congregants clap. There are a few "Amen"s. My legs start to shake. We are never going to see eye to eye. I am the wolf in sheep's clothing. I am here to confess, and to add my voice to the minority, even if it's a minority of one. Tobias puts his hand on my quivering thigh, and I move away. I feel sick.

I hesitantly raise my hand, unsure of how you ask to address a congregation. Women don't speak in this church. They aren't elders or deacons. They don't serve communion. They aren't called on to pray. The last time I was in front of the entire church was the Christmas program when I was in seventh grade. I was too old, and didn't want to get onstage with the plump-skinned youngsters playing out the nativity scene. But they needed more angels. Just before we were to file onstage, I got my first period. Mary and Joseph and even the wise men were scandalized by the blood on my white gown. I ran into the cold choir room and hid in the big box of angel costumes, burrowing under the cheap sheets and tinseled halos.

"Minister Swain, there's something I need to say. May I go first?"

"Why yes, Rachel. You, after all, may understand what Tom is going through more than anyone."

Help me, I think, maneuvering out of the pew and up the aisle. *Save me.* Why am I back here? The slow walk to the front of the church is like a journey to the gallows. I focus on holding my head up, looking straight ahead, and my eyes rest on a giant hand that grips a cane in the aisle. The hand is scrubbed clean though it bears the marks of farm work, of honest labor. Honest hands, hard hearts. I lift my eyes from the hand on the cane to the face of the farmer. Hawk Leach, a man known for his huge appetite and his love of children. I realize I have stopped in the center of the aisle as the congregation watches and waits. I resent them for judging me, but I have judged them, too. I want to run, but I force myself to move forward, toward the sanctuary, the church's sanctuary, my witness stand.

Standing in front of the communion table, where Lily lay days before, I again feel like the seventh grader in my soiled gown.

"Many of you know that in 1985, when I was eleven, my brother, Garland, and I were with Minister Swain's son, Rufus, when he was shot and killed in the woods."

Roberta shivers, frowning. When she sees me looking at her, she forces her grimace into a smile. It is one of the worst moments of my life. She is forcing herself to smile at me, the way ministers' wives must swallow their own pain and desires to reassure and comfort the rest of us.

"What you don't know is that Garland didn't shoot Rufus. It was unintentional, but I'm the one who pulled the trigger."

No one challenges me. There is only silence. I want to run down the aisle, to rewind time, to push past the men guarding the door. I press on in a rush.

"The three of us were playing, and Professor was killed. I killed him. I need you to know that this death was both accidental and unforgivable. Now Tom, too, will go through life with this terrible burden."

I look out and can almost feel their anger, rolling toward me, like waves bringing a dead animal ashore.

"I've been told that guns are a necessary tradition here. That the rituals of hunting are passed down from father to son through the generations, and that this tradition must be protected. This is a small community, and yet, Lily is not the first child who has been shot to death. I am asking how many dead children this tradition is worth. And I ask you to remember that one day the child sacrificed may be your own."

"It was an accident!" Tom's father shouts, half standing, gripping the back of the pew.

"I'm not disputing that."

"You're twisting a tragedy into something else," Earl says, from the other side of the aisle.

"A kindergartener is dead from a gunshot. That's a fact."

"It's no one's fault. It could have happened to anyone."

"That's not—" I begin to respond, but am cut off.

"Don't you think Tom is going through enough?" Tilly says, standing beside her husband, who is shaking with anger. "Don't you think this family is suffering?"

"Of course you are," I say, and my voice shakes because I hadn't planned on arguing with Tom's grieving mother. But I have to speak as someone who has caused that same grief.

"And you want to prevent another family suffering in the same way."

"You've gone off and got fancy ideas. And you think you're going to tell us how to live. You have no say here."

Minister Swain looks uncomfortable. He comes toward me, but Roberta stifles a squeak, like a mouse being stepped on by a big, blind foot. He shakes his head, and goes to her.

"The gall of you coming here and telling Tom's parents they should be charged, when your own parents weren't charged thirty years ago," says a voice from a middle row. I see the man speaking, but I can't place him. "Everything was just fine for your family."

"My own parents weren't charged, but I can tell you everything was not fine with my family. And Tom's parents won't go to prison and orphan him when he's suffering. They might be fined. There might be community service and probation. This is about precedent, not vengeance. No one is coming for your hunting rifles."

"It's a slippery slope!" Earl shouts. "It starts with one restriction and ends with a bunch of defenseless sheep."

"It's not slippery," I retort, losing any sense of calm or clarity. "There's no slope! We live in the flats." I'm at a total loss for words. I look at the crowd, and may as well be a middle schooler, sweating in my long velvet Sears, Roebuck Christmas dress.

"You have no right. You left and got educated beyond your intelligence," says a woman in the middle row. That phrase is something I have heard before, the cry of the wounded. Their pain has obliterated both the cause and the cure. "You hardly came home to see your poor parents. And, if what you say is true, you let your own brother take the blame. Maybe if you'd taken responsibility, your brother wouldn't have killed himself."

The breath has been knocked out of me. I sputter. "I'm not talking about taking guns from adults, I'm talking about taking them from children. Isn't there something between guns for all and guns for none?"

"We are Church of Christ Christians," Lee Ann Olson says. She's always been unbearably righteous, but her only son died two years ago from a drug overdose. She claims it was a random heart attack. "We are not halfway people. We don't believe in purgatory. There's heaven, and there's hell."

"The two of us in this room who killed a child are already in hell. Does it make you feel virtuous to look down on us burning in our own guilt? Is that what you would wish on your own child?"

"Don't talk about my child! You're not even a mother. What do you know about anything?"

Tom walks up the aisle, erect and formal, and there's a rustle in the pews. He goes into the choir room, and comes out holding his shotgun. A collective breath is sucked in as though the old church itself is inhaling hard and loud. Two men rise and call, not to Tom, who walks to the front of the church, but to the armed men guarding the doors.

I am paralyzed in place before the table. *This do in remembrance of me.* We are all stunned into stillness, as the men with concealed weapons run up the aisle.

"Tom! Put that down."

Tom does not turn back, but walks steadily toward the front of the church, straight-backed and silent.

"Tom!" Calvin shouts, running with his gun drawn, pointed at a child.

Tom lays his rifle on the communion table, and without a word, turns down the center aisle and walks out of the church. There are moments of the deep silence of shock or prayer before Tilly runs out, followed by Burl, who slams the church door.

Calvin quickly replaces his gun in its holster and perches awkwardly at the end of the nearest pew. People squeeze down to give him room. A couple of men pat him on the back.

I somehow find my way back to my seat. The gun lies on the communion table and no one makes a move.

Minister Swain lumbers up the steps to the pulpit and tries to recover, beginning what must be a draft of this week's sermon. Maybe he has someone's attention, but I am barely aware of what he is saying. We all look at him from our pews, rigid and empty-eyed. My unseeing gaze travels to the ceiling, where the water stains I saw years ago as animal shapes have fed and expanded, and I'm wondering how I ever saw a lion and a cub when clearly it's a hunter and a doe.

The minister's voice changes, shakes, as he tells us we should continue the gun discussion when tempers have cooled. He pivots to a sermon on Shiloh, and how in the book of Joshua it's a place of rest, a place of assembly, and in Jeremiah it's a place of evil and is destroyed. The New Testament doesn't mention Shiloh at all. That's why a lot of people haven't heard of it, he says.

"But here, we study the Old Testament with the New. Friends, how is it that a place can be two things at once? A holy place and a place of evil? Is our Shiloh the Shiloh of Joshua or of Jeremiah? Maybe it's time to think about change.

I hate change. Most of us here do. I'm embarrassed to tell you the other day I had the thought that I even dislike when the seasons change because the bugs come inside. And as summer fades to fall, it brings me closer to the season of my son's death."

He is trembling now, and he stops speaking. Two deacons go to him and lead him down from the pulpit, one on either side, like guards flanking a condemned man. The organist plays a lackluster hymn.

People file out, and I sit stiff, with closed eyes. Tobias tries to take my hand, but I brush him off. When I leave, troubled and alone, Vasta is the only one in the churchyard. She touches her neck, and I glimpse the port stain that stretches below her ear toward her collarbone. I used to stare at it in church, wondering if it granted her supernatural powers. I was that sort of rude and dreamy child. I move toward her, a severe, almost elegant figure, but she nods curtly and walks away.

SEVENTEEN

THE PHONE IS ringing as I enter the house. It stops just as I pick up. As soon as I leave the kitchen, it starts ringing again. I'm uneasy. Maybe because the house phone seldom rings. Even though reception is bad, everyone I know calls my cell phone, with my New York number that I may never give up.

"Hello?"

There is static on the line, and I'm chilled, remembering Roberta's encounter with Rufus. Would the dead use a telephone?

"Is someone there?"

"Lady, can you come get your dog?"

"Is she dead?"

"Dead? Heck no, she's a mess, driving us up the wall. She's blatting like a baby, getting the other animals all worked up. I mean, we don't expect it quiet, but this is, well, listen for yourself."

The voice goes away. The caller must be holding the

receiver up; I hear the cacophony of sad, imprisoned animals, and June's howl loudest of all.

"You hear it?" she asks, coming back on the line. "Your dog doesn't have rabies. She's healthy and homesick. Please come as quick as you can."

I CAN'T SAY that I've ever been greeted with the enthusiasm June shows me. When the vet's assistant brings her out, June jumps into my arms like a clumsy lover. Her stinky sloppy-tongued kisses are relentless.

At the house, she keeps close, clipping my heels. After much affection and petting and biscuit giving, I try to read on the couch. She nudges my hand with her head, until I must hold the book with one hand and stroke her bony noggin with the other.

"You're the top dog and I'm the dogsbody."

She barks in agreement.

JUNE AND I take long walks on the dirt roads, across the fields and through the woods, until we find ourselves back at the swimming hole, the Red Dredge. I worry she might be traumatized by the memory of the rabid raccoon, but she is in her ever-happy ever-present, bounding into the water without a care.

The memory of baptizing Professor comes to me, as clear and vivid as the here and now. I wade in, tugging his hand and pulling him beside me. The warm water laps our waists, and Professor says we don't need to go so deep. "You know I can't swim, Rachel."

"Can you taste the sin bitter on your tongue?" I cry, as the revival preacher used to shout, flinging sweat and judgment. "Don't you want to be washed in the blood of the lamb?"

"You're going to dunk me, aren't you?" Professor asks, with a sigh.

"Don't you want to be saved? Are you ready? Because it weren't raining when Noah built that ark."

I push him under and tell him to hold his nose. I bring him up, drunk on my power, and tell him how light he is in the water. I ask him if he repents his sins. "Yes," he says, "yes." Then I push him under again and tug his hair to hold him down. He paddles his hands in the air and rises, gasping. He rubs his eyes, stands up straight and squeezes my hand. "I think I saw."

"Saw what? You know you can't see without your glasses."

"You don't need glasses to see God," he says solemnly.

JUNE GUARDS THE area while I climb into Garland's deer stand. It's the old plywood style, and, at seven by four feet, is big enough to stand up in, a small room in the trees.

An unread novel waits in my book bag, an old flour sack taken from the garden shed. I've been reading articles and what environmental writing I can find about farming. How the chemicals—pesticides, fertilizers, and growth regulators— might affect drinking water sources as a result of run-off. How tobacco depletes soil nutrients by taking up more nitrogen, phosphorous, and potassium than other major crops. How the depletion is compounded by topping and suckering plants, which increases the nicotine content of the leaves. I remember with churning emotions how I loved the long, spiked pink flowers that sprouted from the top of these nightshades, plants of sorcery and witchcraft, of poison and, here, of lifeblood. Tobacco is dead here, in this county anyway. If the land can change and adapt, why can't we.

AT THE EDGE of the deer stand, I point my toes over the edge and close my eyes, as we used to dare each other in childhood—me, Garland, Professor. I could step the closest without falling off, though one time I did. My rubbery child's bones didn't break, and we never told. I stand, suspended, feeling slightly dizzy, wondering what happened to the fierce girl I used to be, when I see something move through the trees, near the swimming hole. Four people are walking toward the water—two white men, a white woman, and a Black man I've never seen before. Instinctively I crouch down, and lying on my belly, I have a clear view of the foursome framed by the tree leaves. Cobb and Elton, the men's names come to me as in a dream. They're mean and rough and children have been told to stay away from them, an unnecessary warning. They're pushing the other two with their rifles—Cobb has his rifle at the woman's back, and Elton rests his on the shoulder of the Black man. At the edge of the water, the woman pauses, and Cobb pushes her harder with the rifle. He says something, but I can't hear, which is odd because sound travels so easily over water, and voices carry. She's crying and I *do* hear him say, with the rifle raised, If you turn around I'll kill you. So she walks into the water. She hesitates, and takes off her shoes. Nothing else. Just her shoes, a sight that pierces me as I see them sitting empty on the bank. Then she walks into the water, fully clothed just as I had seen Annie Gurkin do at a river baptism years ago, as she walked carefully into the Tar

River, while we sang "Blest Be the Tie that Binds" from the shore. But now I watch the woman in the brown dress with roses on it as she continues walking into the dredge as the water licks her slip, which is hanging down below her dress on the left side. I watch, paralyzed with panic, as though I have fallen out of time. The man is being prodded with the other rifle, and he reaches out to the woman and they clasp hands. Luther, she says, very clearly. The man bangs him on the shoulder with the rifle. He turns back and is shot in the face. I begin to scream without seeming to make any sound.

"Rachel," someone calls, "Rachel!" and I look down to see Vasta Gurkin, peering up at me through the leaves.

"Vasta. I don't know what's happening," I say, scrambling down the ladder. "I must be hallucinating. A man was shot," I point at the water, my arm shaking.

"I've been here an hour," she says. "No one was shot, not today. Although a man was killed here years ago, a woman, too."

"Here?"

"Why do you think they call it the Red Dredge?"

"Because it was created with a dredge."

Vasta shakes her head. "They used to call it the swimming hole. It got the name Red Dredge in the forties, after it was dredged for two bodies."

I'm shuddering now, and June is hugging my leg, looking from me to Vasta.

"Are you saying what I saw is something that really happened, years ago, before I was born?"

"Why not? The shape of the past is in the present here. If you pay attention, you'll see all kinds of things."

She follows me to the water, and I point, speechless. "There."

"The angel of history."

"That was no angel."

"Figure of speech," she says, "the ghost of history, one of many. Let me show you something."

She leads me to a spot in the beech trees, and kneels by a log. She begins scratching in the dirt. "Do you know the story of the Witch Bride?" she asks.

"The one who slips her skin at night?"

She looks up at me from her crouch, her hand on an old stone slab that we used to play on as children.

"It's a ghost story, Vasta. You don't believe a witch was really flying around at night."

"No. It wasn't a witch. It was a woman. My great great great grandmother. This is where they buried her."

"You're saying the Witch Bride is a story about a real woman, and that she's buried here, and she's your ancestor."

"Yes."

She stands, brushing her hands and pinning me in place with her clear eyes.

"Is she still buried there?"

"No, the body's gone. Some of my family had her exhumed and moved to the family plot years ago. But this is where they buried her, after she was poisoned."

"That's hard to believe, Vasta."

"Still, it happened. She was a midwife, and one winter three babies died in delivery. She was also independent, and liked to move freely. She was accused of bewitching a man and killing his wife and infant. Her husband distrusted her going off to deliver babies in the middle of the night. So he poisoned her, and the town sanctioned her murder."

"I thought it was just a ghost story, like they have everywhere."

"Virginia Dare and Theodosia Burr are in the same book of North Carolina ghost stories. They were real people."

"And Joe Brooks."

"Yes."

"So you think we tell ourselves ghost stories about history we can't face."

"Sometimes it's to justify our atrocities. Sometimes to scare ourselves. Other places might be different. I thought this was your field of study."

"I never thought about it this way. I mean I thought about what the stories were doing, the morality lessons, especially for girls, and I thought of the Witch Bride as one of those, a warning story about a woman punished for her self-possession and disobedience."

"What's interesting to me," Vasta says, "is how the stories have stopped."

"Have they?"

"You're the scholar."

"That doesn't seem to help." I don't say that I've always been a little ashamed of my field of study, and only here have I finally understood that's in part what attracted me: I belonged to the fringe, to the obsolescent. "I used to think because it's a form of oral history, that sort of tradition, moralizing and warped and nostalgic as it may be, is a bridge to the past that people don't want to be reminded of anymore."

"And now?"

"Being here has made me wonder if these tales were created to exist outside history. And maybe we've decided we do, too. Maybe we are the folktale. Maybe we are the ghost story."

BY THE OLD collapsed barn, something has dug up the first wolf, or coywolf, whatever it was. A wake of vultures harvest scraps from the carcass, intent on their work and not pausing as June and I approach. Suddenly, a bald eagle swoops overhead and buzzes us, but the vultures will not quit their work. They beat their wings in a fury until the eagle flies up and dive-bombs again. The standoff continues until the eagle comes so close, we feel the air disturbed by his whipping wings, and the protesting vultures take flight like a dark and feathery tornado. The eagle stands beside the carcass, unfazed by my presence. We are side by side, eyeing the skeleton, a few tatty patches of fur clinging to bone. That is all that is left. I have the inexplicable urge to reach for a bone, and as I do, the eagle looks me—bang—in the eye, as though to remind me of my place. I may take only what the eagle allows.

I am still holding a femur when I meet Palmer on the road. He nods, looks down at my hand, and I feel that I should explain, but cannot.

"Souvenir?"

"It's from one of these wolf-like animals that are dying. The vultures were picking it clean, until an eagle came and took over."

"You took a leg?"

"I don't know why."

"Southerners like their souvenirs."

"Oh, Palmer," I say, dropping the bone in the road.

"Palmer, you know why they call the swimming hole the Red Dredge?"

"Yes, I know why. Do you?"

"Because a red walking dredge rotted there years ago."

"That's not it. There was a man, Luther Smallwood, but they called him Red. They found his body in there, a woman's, too. They'd been shot."

"Was it an accident?"

"They say it was a double suicide."

"Do you believe that?"

"There were a lot more 'suicides' in those days than there were people who killed themselves."

EIGHTEEN

SHE MARCHES UP the drive, military straight, carrying a black patent leather purse.

Vasta as a visitor is a surprise. I'm sure she has a purpose.

"Nice to see you again," I say, inviting her inside, not mentioning but recalling the scene at the Dredge, which now seems to belong to some uncertain tertiary world. I don't know how to speak of it, so I say instead, "I almost spoke to you at Lily's funeral."

"An infuriating funeral for an unnecessary death," she says, stepping inside. "Then they turned around and had a Second Amendment meeting."

"Would you like tea?"

"I'll take coffee if you've got it," she says.

She smooths her cotton skirt with one hand and, with the other, places the shiny purse on the table. It's either new or unused, and seeing Vasta with it is almost as unexpected as her presence in my parents' kitchen.

As I make coffee she sits upright on the edge of her chair, tracing the grain of the table wood with her long, supple fingers.

"Are you still teaching porcelain painting?" I ask, getting out the pink depression coffee mugs my mother saved for special visitors.

"I couldn't take those little hoodlums any longer. They were rough and restless and loud. The Dixon boy was angry with me after I boxed his ears for spilling paint. We're only here 'cause they make us! he shouted and called me an old spinster. I picked up the drop cloth by its four edges, dumped the whole mess, and told the children to get out."

"I'm sorry, Vasta."

"Don't be. It's much better with just us in the house, the three little pigs."

I look at her in surprise.

"Yes, we know. What do we care?"

She waves away sugar and cream, and stirring her black coffee says, "I guess you're wondering why I'm here."

"You're welcome anytime."

"You and I have something in common. We both killed someone."

My legs liquefy and I sink into the chair opposite her. She is entirely unshakeable, her expression serene, her face full of mystery.

"I guess everyone knows about me, since I told the entire church."

"I doubt anyone was surprised about your confession."

I feel weightless, hypnagogic, and touch the table to make sure I'm here and that Vasta is not an apparition.

"It's a shame my family kept the lie all these years," I finally manage. "In the end, it seems we're the only ones who believed in it."

"Your parents were good people, humble and private. But neighbors sometimes know you better than you think."

"So I'm learning."

She looks at me with her long oval face, the face of a seventeenth-century Madonna, or the Witch Bride's descendant.

"I almost went off to the teacher's college in Raleigh. But mother was ill, and Pearl and Annie were too young to take care of themselves, much less her. I couldn't leave them here with *him*. So I stayed."

"Your father was—"

"My father was an ogre and a brute. He lost half our acreage, and he almost lost it all. He would have, too, if we didn't stop him."

I don't know what to say. She opens the purse, with its tight silver twist clasp, and removes an antique pistol, which she places carefully on the table.

"Don't worry. It's not loaded."

"I don't understand."

"We couldn't keep him away from Annie—I'm sure you know about that."

"It's none of my business."

"You're not in New York anymore. Other people's business is the business here. There's no need to dredge up the details, except to say if you ever need to get rid of something, lye is extremely effective."

"I think drug cartels use it to break down bodies."

"Well, tried and true. Anyway, I admired the way Tom

turned in his shotgun at the town meeting. I hear you've given up your guns, too. So I thought I'd add another to the pile."

"I'm not collecting weapons."

"You should. Gather them up. Everyone won't do it. Maybe none of the men. But there are others."

"Why me? I don't know what to do with them."

"The sheriff's office will take them. And you're the best candidate for collection. You're not a stranger, but you're not a local either."

"What am I then?"

"You tell me," she says, and stands to go, so I don't answer. "I'm not much for chit chat, Rachel. And I've been wanting to get rid of this gun for a long time, since the once I used it."

"Aren't you worried about getting caught?"

She shrugs. "Everybody knew he went off on his drunken binges at the horse races. One time he made a bad deal and he didn't come back."

"People believe that?"

She looks at me like my father used to when I came home with a 100 in statistics and then forgot how to calibrate the seed drill.

"People here aren't daft. There's the story we tell ourselves that we want to believe and there's what we know to be true."

I might be the most educated least knowledgeable soul in Shiloh. "And you're trusting me?"

"I've been trusting your family a long time. Your father loaned us some . . . Let's say he taught us about toxicity. He always gave what we asked to borrow. He turned over our fields and helped us around the place. Tobias, too."

Her smile softens her severe face. "My sister Pearl and I

have started a reading group, if you'd like to join. It's just the two of us, but we take it seriously."

"Thank you. I've really missed talking about literature. What are you reading?"

"*Critique of Pure Reason.*"

"Oh."

"We're country, Rachel. We're not illiterate."

"I never thought that."

"Wednesday mornings, nine sharp. We concentrate on a paragraph at a time, sometimes a sentence. Like Bible study. We're on section two, the 'Transcendental Exposition of the Conception of Time.'"

"I'll be there."

She stands to go but pauses, touching her port stain and looking at me steadily with frank, unblinking eyes.

"Do you have a favorite? Of the stories you study."

"It began with the Witch Bride."

"How do you write about it?"

"Poorly. I've been thinking of trying a new way, but I haven't been able to."

"Why don't you try telling the story in your own words?"

I shift, uncomfortable and exposed, as she stands looking at me with her truth-serum gaze. "You mean like a fictional story? I've wanted to, but I can't."

"Why not?"

"I'm stuck. Maybe I'm waiting for permission."

"That sounds like an excuse."

I don't answer, but move toward the door and wait for her to leave. On her way out she turns back. "Do you know why they call us the three little pigs?"

"Because you walk down the road in single file."

"No, that's what they tell children. They call us the three little pigs because we took care of the big, bad wolf."

She walks confidently down the drive, the black purse perched in the crook of her arm like a cat. I'd be honored to call her a friend, and I wouldn't cross her for a million bucks.

I sit at the table with my books and broken thoughts. If we are the folktales, we should write a new reality.

THE HOUSE IS quiet after Vasta's presence, and I rattle around on my own, like a ghost, opening doors and finding nothing to haunt. I flip through my books on the kitchen table, the essays and articles, ripping up journals and throwing them in recycling. I go outside, jog around the house, kick rocks in the drive, and before I can change my mind, I run inside, sit at the table and write without stopping.

THE WITCH BRIDE

She waits until he sleeps. It does not take long. He is a hard-used farmer, and he falls asleep quickly after the exercise of early marriage. Then she sheds her skin and flies away.

It is dazzling in the starry sky, soaring over the pine-lands and tobacco fields in the humid night scented with fresh grass and overturned earth. She does no harm, watching over this sleepy hamlet where life is short but full of hours. There is always the land to work: setting out, putting in, sheeting up.

She sights the rare red wolves, her nocturnal soul mates, and hovers above them, overseeing the hunt for rabbits or raccoons, or, on a lucky night, a deer.

Near dawn, she slips back inside the house and calls softly to the flesh she left behind:

"Skin, skin, you know me?

"Skin, skin, this is me."

She reunites with her body and lies down gently beside her husband. It goes on like this, for days, weeks, months, until her husband becomes rough, terse, watchful. She is an excellent farmer's wife, helpful in the house and the fields, in all the rooms and all the rows. But it is not enough.

He meets with men of the town, and explains how his wife disappears at night and returns before dawn. One of the men, a grizzled old farmer whose terror in life is being stranded without chew, says the wife is a witch. The husband is to search the house at night, and see if she has shed her skin. Look under the stairs, he says.

Sure enough, that night when he pretends to sleep and the wife disappears, he finds her flesh in a heap under the stairs. He does as instructed, peppering the skin as though heavily seasoning a hide. He first sprinkles the spice, then takes to vigorous rubbing, through the torso, the legs, the empty little feet, then back up, in the arm sleeves down to the tapered fingertips.

Upstairs, just before dawn, he hears her soft, spellbinding voice:

"Skin, skin, you know me?

"Skin, skin, this is me."

She slips into bed beside him, and he edges away in horror. Within minutes she is sweating and tossing, scratching and moaning. "Skin," she whispers, "this is—" but her husband has destroyed her from the inside. She is unintelligible within the hour, and neighbors stop by to watch her death, which comes that evening, after great suffering. She is buried with haste and recited scripture in the woods, under a stand of trees, known as Big Beech Island, though it is not big, has no water, nor any qualities of an island. She is buried not with care or mourning, but so she will be far from the townspeople. They place a slab of stone over the grave so she can't escape, as witches are wont to do.

Her mother and sisters come in the middle of the night to take her home (they have traveled far; her people are not from here, the locals always made a point to mention), but they cannot budge the stone. She lies there still, in an unmarked, unvisited tomb.

I've never written anything as swiftly, and I don't look at it, but leave the table invigorated. There is no witch, no woman, who can't be brought back, resurrected in some form at least, on the page. Finally, a passion project. It's not about studying these stories in books, but about entering the world of these metamorphosed women. It's about entering their world through a door I imagine.

I'M SUDDENLY INTERESTED in my mother's kitchen, and I open the cupboards as though it's a stranger's house. There are old cans of Vienna sausages, jars of pepper vinegar and sticky molasses. I need to start categorizing, organizing, de-past-iz-ing. I have to "put things to rights." The phrase is something my mother might say. My parents are the only ones who were ever truly comfortable in this house, and I can almost imagine them still here. Dad's outside somewhere, unseen, but carefully tending to whatever needs tending. Stepping inside the dark cool of the living room, I see the scrap quilt my mother used when she napped on the couch. It's hanging there now, and I can almost see her sleeping with her mouth open. I look down at this aging stranger and know if I were to say, "Mom, are you sleeping?" she would blink and struggle up and say, "No, I was just resting my eyes. Do you need anything?"

It was one of my visits last year when she told me that members of her Bible study group were going to dress up as women in Scripture, and asked me to come. There had been a brief tiff because two of them wanted to be Mary. I had unhelpfully pointed out that there are half a dozen Marys in the Bible. Someone could be Virgin Mary, and someone could be another Mary, the fallen one, the one who washed Jesus' feet with her hair.

"You know no one wants to be the fallen Mary," my mother said.

"Why not? She's redeemed. Anyway, the faithful need whores. They need Madonnas and they need whores."

Why had I cut her with my causticism? She thought I was making fun of her, that I was ashamed. There was something about the reenactments that especially frayed my agnostic nerves.

I went with her, reluctantly, and sat like a corrupt anthropologist in Jackie White's carpeted living room. I was the only one not wearing a sheet or a towel or a robe. Someone asked who I was, and before I could speak, my mother blurted out that I was Lot's wife. It was then that I realized I embarrassed my mother, or, rather, I realized she was embarrassed by me.

I recalled with pain how I had been embarrassed when I was in college in New York. I didn't bring friends home because I didn't want them to see how rural we were.

During the Bible study, which was, interestingly, on Hagar and Ishmael, I studied my mother's friends. They knew exactly which biblical woman they wanted to be, and they knew exactly who they were—somebody's wife, somebody's mother. Sitting on hard cane chairs in a circle, I felt silly that I had always resented motherhood. Being unattached to anything, utterly alone as I was, was quite hard, and perhaps had changed me in ways that were just as bad as belonging to others and not fully to yourself. As I sat there among the biblical women, every one of them married, every one of them mothers, I thought of how hard it must be for my own mother, who probably wanted a different daughter, one who married and gave her grandchildren. The precarious academic life I had constructed for myself was as much a fantasy and unattached to reality as these women portraying women of the Bible.

But in my heart of hearts, I didn't believe that.

A few months after Bible study, I went to Paris with Lucas. We took a long walk and wandered into Sainte-Chapelle, the gothic masterpiece, with its soaring panels of stained glass where Biblical stories were depicted in brilliant color. Lot's wife was there, and the sight of her, the only glass pane absent of color, a pillar of salt against the surrounding brightness, left me shaken. She was a clear column, not a ghost but a statue. Had she turned back with longing or regret? I had always been taught that Lot's wife was turned into a pillar of salt because she was disobedient; she was told not to look back and she did it anyway. Of course the part where Lot offers up his two virgin daughters to be gang-raped instead of the male strangers he's housing was glossed over. But why had Lot's wife, the woman without a name, refused to follow? What if failing to flee had been her escape from servitude? The curatorial cards in English were taken, so Lucas and I tried the Italian translation. It was surprising how little I remembered of many of the stories. My mother would have recognized them, known them, and she would have found the room undeniably beautiful. I should have gone to Europe with her, not Lucas, and now it's too late. She'll never see the stained glass of Sainte-Chapelle, and I'll never know why she called me Lot's wife.

NINETEEN

I CALL TO invite Jewel to dinner again and she hesitates at another invitation, "so soon," she murmurs. "It's been more than two weeks!" I say, emphatically, and then, more gently, "I'd love to see Lyric, and I owe you since I burned our first dinner."

When they arrive I stop myself from rushing out to the car to greet them. The table is set; the tuna salad is ready. I'm determined to keep it simple and do it right this time. It's too hot to cook, and oil-packed tuna and late summer vegetables are easily found, even here.

I take Lyric while Jewel puts down her bag, washes her hands.

"Can I see Garland's room again?"

I nod, and Lyric puts her head against my chest, forehead first, in what I realize is a movement particular to her, and has nothing to do with me. I take her outside where she is immediately bitten by a mosquito. I automatically pop the insect on her arm, spraying blood and shocking this twice-injured baby. She looks at me with suspicion and I run inside with her, frightened of my own incompetence.

Opening the kitchen drawer for ointment, I see Vasta's pistol between the masking tape and a ball of twine. I slam the drawer shut. I had forgotten! And here I am, dangling a baby above a gun. I jostle Lyric with one hand and grip the counter with the other.

"What's wrong?" Jewel asks, coming to stand behind me.

"There are still guns in the house. Unloaded, but I'd forgotten. Children are not safe here!"

She takes Lyric from me, and drapes another of Garland's T-shirts over the tiny shoulders. She's scared for Lyric, I think, and it's like burning nettles brushing my heart. Be careful, I tell myself. Don't be crazy. Don't make her afraid to have Lyric visit.

"What makes children safe?" she asks, calm and even.

"Houses without guns for one thing."

"You're in rural North Carolina. You're back for three weeks and you're going to take on gun control?"

"I'm not stupid. But look at what Tom is going through. Until there are—"

"Do you really know what it's like for Tom? You sound more like a hypocrite than a helper. You killed a child and let your brother take the blame. It destroyed him. And you, you're still here, with a farm to yourself and no one to depend on you. So you've got time to tell us how we don't live right."

Lyric, attuned to our tone, looks at us, from one to the other, her face serious, alert to danger.

"I'm not proselytizing. I mean I am. But I'm not saying

guns should be banned. They should be kept from kids. Is that unreasonable?"

Jewel lowers her voice for Lyric's sake, soothing both of us. "Why are you taking this on, Rachel?"

"Sometimes we have to live as though the world is how we want it to be," I say, surprising myself.

"I never figured you for an idealist."

"Jewel, I want to do better. Garland had stopped speaking to me years ago, and I figured no one would believe me. You know how people here are. Once they believe something, they never change their minds. Everyone believed it was Garland. I didn't see how I could change that."

"You think you've been deceiving us all these years. Is that it?"

"Yes."

"Why can't you understand, Rachel? People here *know*. They know about Palmer, and about Joe Brooks. They know Joe Brooks was lynched. They know about you and about Garland. They know who you are, who you were, what you did. But they're never going to say it because they don't want to and they don't have to. People here don't not know the past. They can't live here and not know it. Believe you me, they *know*."

"All this time, we lived a lie for nothing." I slide to the floor, leaning against the cupboards, wanting to crawl inside. I have judged all the people here, thinking I was somehow apart.

"Hey," Jewel says. "Let's not fall apart in front of Lyric." I nod and slowly, carefully, move to the table. "I want to ease her out of her innocence. They sense our stress. Remember that."

We eat dinner quietly and I wish I'd prepared something

better. As we're clearing the plates, Lyric lifts her head and looks at me, straight on, as a jolt passes through my body.

"May I hold her?"

I take her from Jewel, and she comes willingly, as far as I can tell. We go out on the porch and I settle on the swing with her. I wish they would stay the night, or forever. Jewel keeps me in line, and Lyric keeps me in love. I hadn't realized how much I'd missed both.

"The historical society in Raleigh had an exhibit last year, when a book on lynching was published. Garland and I went to see it with Palmer. And there was my great-grandfather, Joe Brooks, under glass. Can you imagine?"

"No."

"It was a postcard. You could stamp it and send it like a letter to be delivered anywhere in the world."

"Christ," I whisper.

"He might have been there, too," she says. "It was like white church. All those people, a congregation, to see a man strung up. They had a photographer and turned it into souvenirs."

"A lynching postcard."

"Your grandfather was there. Palmer recognized him. He looked like a normal boy, perched on his father's shoulders, both in white short-sleeve shirts, your grandfather had gold round-framed glasses and looked as calm as could be."

"My grandfather was at your great grandfather's murder?"

"Say lynching."

"Lynching. Jewel—"

"Don't tell me you're sorry or you feel bad or whatever it is, don't say it. The thing is, he looked like Garland. He looked like you. He looked like your whole family."

I hold Lyric closer. "We live in disgrace."

"Speak for yourself," Jewel says, and takes Lyric.

"I didn't mean you. I meant—"

"I know what you mean, but it doesn't matter. It's time for us to go," she says abruptly.

"Please stay. You can go through Garland's things. I'll watch Lyric."

"Give this time, Rachel."

I hug Lyric and offer my services as a babysitter, which I know sounds idiotic.

"Look, Rachel. I know you're not your grandfather. But he *was* your grandfather. And I know you're sorry about Garland, but you didn't tell the truth. Like I said earlier, people here know things, but they don't always acknowledge them. They don't atone. And you're who you are, where you're from, and, honest, you've ignored some history yourself."

"I'm not going anywhere. I'm going to learn to live here."

"Damn earnest white people," Jewel says, as I watch them closely, trying to assess my chances. "That expression reminds me of Garland."

"Is that good?"

"It's good," she says, and ducks inside the car to explore the mysteries of infant carseats, while I hold Lyric, caressing her head. My fingers accidentally brush her fontanel, and I shudder at how defenseless she is, with this soft spot in her skull that could be fatal. At the same time, nothing in her life is irreversible—yet.

The thing about a fontanel is that it eventually closes up. We're born whole but unfinished, with skulls that must harden like shells. It takes time. The thing about a photograph is what's in the frame is never unfinished and can never be undone.

TEARS ON MY face and a sob in my throat. It's as though ghosts are correcting me in whispers and echoes. I close my eyes to sleep, and see the deer, the deer with two heads wearing Professor's face. I see Joe Brooks, walking the tracks. I see the wolf, always watching. But when I open my eyes I only see Lyric.

On the last night I saw my parents alive, we ate supper without speaking. They were lonelier when I was here. I was a reminder that hurled us all into our shared memory, which we did not want because we were not a sharing family and memories were an unbearable burden. When I left, they could continue their life as a couple, almost as though they never had children at all.

It is terrible for solitary people to be bound the way we were, bound by a lie. That the most important event of our lives was something that happened to us together left each of us riven inside. Garland took the blame, and then he cleaved us from his life.

Without him, I am truly alone. That's how Lucas broke things off. You're a lone wolf, he said. You have a solitary quality that makes you intriguing at first, and impossible long term.

Success and failure are beginning to seem ornamental; maybe I can survive here. I don't need archives to witness to Southern history; it is before me, visible everywhere. I've been hiding from it. I can look out at the field, can drive around this provincial village. I can talk to Vasta or to Palmer on his rounds.

"Don't dwell," my father said. He also said, "A man can't live everywhere." In the sixteenth century the condemned were often executed on the site where the crime was committed. That seems right. I won't be executed, but I must stay near the scene.

I FINALLY GO through the rest of the house, searching these strange yet familiar nooks, stopping at the bookcase in the living room. It's hardwood, nothing fancy, but sturdy, stained dark, with curved legs and a glass front that as a child I loved to slide open and closed. On the bottom shelf, the *World Book Encyclopedia* rests, spine out, in its sepulcher, our altar to Professor. How my mother scrimped and saved for that set, taking up bookkeeping for the wealthy owner of the local lumber company. Garland and I would groan when we asked a question and she would inevitably say, "Let's look in the *World Book*." But I secretly loved it, and pored over the pages, especially the entry on the human body, with its transparent layers revealing the body's skeletal, digestive, circulatory, reproductive, and nervous systems. I lifted the pages again and again for the sticky sound, and the sight of the body's inner systems revealed. "The body starts out as one cell. In time, this tiny cell develops into a body consisting of trillions of cells. The human body can also replace certain worn-out parts. . . . Every 15 to 30 days, for instance, the human body replaces the outermost layer of skin."

The top page of clear plastic still shows two human figures, and I lift each page, revealing the skeletal system, the muscular system, the digestive system. The male figure is turned to the side, the female figure faces the viewer. I peel the pages apart, the respiratory system and circulatory system, then the urinary, reproductive, and endocrine systems, and finally, the nervous system. The male continues to primly hide his penis, but the woman stands full on, staring out with her spooky unprotected eyeballs.

Standing with the book in my hand, I glimpse it on top of the bookcase. I know what I have to do; even so, I spend four days avoiding the task. I can't stand doing it, until finally I can't stand not doing it. The afternoon walk to Tom's is hot, and the orphaned horse is damp in my sweaty hand. Crossing the Langleys' porch, I hear voices through the screen door.

"What kind of boy are we raising here?" Burl seems a fitting name for the body behind that voice.

"The only one we have," comes Tilly's anguished response.

I turn to go, but the house has gone still and the floorboards creak my cowardly presence. I'm almost at the steps when the door opens behind me.

"Rachel," Tom says, coming outside.

"Tom!" his mother calls, appearing behind the screen. She leans forward, pulling the door to her, pressing her face against the mesh.

"Who's here?" Burl says, brushing past her. "Oh," he says flatly. "It's you."

Tom stands beside me and we face them together.

"You want to collect our guns?" Tilly asks bitterly. "Because I'm ready to give them to you."

"No, I—"

"The hell you will," Burl says. "Over my dead body."

We pause to absorb this. I can't think of anything to say, so I thrust the stuffed horse toward her. "I came to return this. Lily left it in my car."

She opens the door, taking the dirty horse, whose right ear has been nearly sucked off, into her hands gently, as though it's fragile.

"Tell her!" Burl shouts at me. "These accidents happen! *You* know."

"Why does she know?" Tilly cries, squeezing the horse in her hands. "Because it keeps happening *again*."

They take their yelling inside.

"Can I come to your house?" Tom asks with tears in his eyes.

"If your parents give permission."

"You mean I have to ask them?"

"You probably should."

"Never mind then."

"Come anytime, Tom. Clear it with your parents. I'm sure they're worried about you."

"I don't really think Lily is in heaven," he whispers. "Lily is in the ground."

I sit beside Tom on the steps. Burl slams out of the house, swearing and miserable. He clutches his keys, rubbing bloodshot eyes, then gets in his truck and backs recklessly out of the drive. Tom turns and I see Tilly wavering in the doorway.

"I didn't mean to add to your suffering."

She nods and wipes her eyes. "They're not going to charge us, you'll be sorry to hear."

"No. I should have spoken more carefully."

"I know," she says quietly. "It's not that I disagree, but it won't bring her back."

"It's my fault," Tom says.

"It was an accident," I say, putting my arm around him, repeating what my parents told me. He doesn't respond, and I know it won't help. Guilt won't weigh the difference.

"How's Irma?" I ask Tilly, because I haven't seen her since before the funeral.

She shakes her head. "She's in the hospital. She was already ill, and this," she glances at Tom and stops herself. "I'm angry, Rachel. But I won't stop Tom if it helps him to talk to you."

I'm at a loss. "I meant it as a legal question," I say, inept and struggling. "I see now it's a bigger question, or a different one. I'm not sure the law even matters."

I'm trying to figure out how to continue, when she says emotionally, "The law always matters. But it can't always make things right."

TWENTY

JEWEL CALLS. SHE has an emergency, and needs someone to look after Lyric. She sounds hesitant, and I know I am not her first choice, or even her third. But she's asking and it's a small good thing.

I take Lyric outside, spread a blanket on the grass, and put her on her belly. She looks at me, and laughs, lifting her arms and legs, swimming in the warm air. She has the beautiful, unblemished skin of a bronze sculpture, *Victorious Youth*, maybe. "Good," I whisper, as she gazes at me with her light eyes, so like Garland's. Slender puffs of skin crease either side of her nose, as though her eyes are too heavy, too innocent, too open to life's tragedies. As I lean over her, she flings her arm out and grabs at air with her chubby, dimple-knuckled hand. I instinctively reach for it, and she grasps my finger.

It strikes me that I am watching a person, a being, at the beginning. She is already in the race of life, and wherever the course detours or winds, she will somehow remain this person before me now on a kitten blanket in the grass.

I do the only thing I know to do when I'm overcome. I take her inside and read to her.

"Once upon a time there was a witch who flew away every night."

Skin, skin, you know me?
Skin, skin, this is me.

SHE RIDES MY hip as we walk through the house that finally seems to be giving, to be opening for us. I find myself singing "I Was Born," surprised I remember the lyrics. It's a song my mother used to sing to me, one of the only times I was allowed to sit in her lap, touch her hair. My mother had been a beauty queen, "back when that really meant something," I once overheard someone whisper. She was beautiful in an Ava Gardner way, with dark hair and deep green eyes and a graceful gait. She had taken a job at Thalhimer's department store after high school, in order to save money for the next round of national pageants. My father had found her there—that was the word they both used, "found"—and so she had become a farmer's wife instead of Miss America. My father was handsome, too, with a cleft in his chin, a devil's dimple, and black hair he Dapper Danned when he went to town. My mother told the story of their meeting one afternoon, when my father walked into the Winston-Salem store after a tobacco auction, as though it were inevitable. It was so obvious to her that my father needed looking after and that it had been her sacrifice to accept the job, one without glory or zirconia tiaras. She became a farmer's wife, and despite initial appearances and local gossip, she excelled, at least at crops and cooking. They were the most humble, hard-working people I've ever known.

Lyric gazes up at me with limpid eyes. I lean down and nuzzle her neck. There are so many things that can go wrong, I think, holding her close.

One thing that does go wrong is the diaper change. The first time it ends up around her knees and the second time it cuts into her thighs. I watch a YouTube video as she giggles at my incompetence.

When she finally has a secure nappy, we go back outside to our blanket. A firefly blinks, then another, and another, and it's as magical as it has been since childhood. I can almost hear our flat feet (Garland's, Professor's, mine) slapping the dirt road as we ran after them in summer's late twilight. We shrieked as we caught them, holding them close to our nose and sniffing their distinct lightning-buggy scent. We pinched their lights off, leaving them denuded and dying on the ground, as we smeared their crushed lights on our T-shirts, and ran, glowing, through the dark, briefly bioluminescent. The effect didn't last long, so we killed more, until Professor put a stop to our carnage. He copied out the firefly entry from his encyclopedia, and instructed us, in dramatic detail, about how they flashed to find mates, and we were effectively killing entire generations. I began to cry, and Professor comforted me, thinking I had acquired a tender heart. I was really crying because I was afraid Professor would turn his attention to the entry on mosquitoes and make us stop killing them, too, in which case we would be eaten alive.

I found the fireflies irresistible, and prayed nightly for my urge to kill to be curbed. "They don't live long anyway," I reasoned with Professor and Garland. "And there are always more." There were things we understood to be in short supply (Nike tennis shoes, brand-name cereal, mall money), but lightning bugs were plentiful. "There are so many!" I cried. "So menny menny menny!" But Professor and Garland were not moved, and so we restricted our killing to tobacco worms, which earned us twenty-five cents per corpse.

LYRIC HAS FALLEN ASLEEP, and I sit very still as a lightning bug lands on my leg, closely investigating my knee before flashing off. Fireflies in New York, lightning bugs in North Carolina. First, I scrubbed my speech. Then I scrubbed my life. I lived, like many New Yorkers, as though rural America didn't exist. It didn't help. When the committee rejected my tenure file, they said I was a regionalist whose work was too small-bore. They are probably right. In 2015, exuberant hope is in the air. Maybe we don't need to worry anymore about witch hags and other imagined villains.

"Everyone's gone." I start to cry, and Lyric wakes, her lips trembling along with mine. They sense our stress, Jewel said, so I smile at her, and she smiles back, not knowing, or caring yet, whether I am saint or sinner, or just a woman, aging and uncertain. There is a hint of discomfort on her face, and I tell myself it must be physical, indigestion perhaps, or simply frustration that she can't get up and walk away. As though she has interpreted my thoughts, she twists and tries to push herself up.

"Blest be the infant Babe," I whisper. "Infant of the universe."

She goes down on her belly, lifting her arms and legs, a tiny superwoman, her eyes bright and watchful.

WHEN JEWEL COMES to take Lyric home, I linger by the car until Jewel says, "Rachel, I need to tell you: To me, you're a liar, from a family of liars. Garland was the best of you."

"He was. I know."

"I'm glad it's been said."

"Jewel, I should never have allowed Garland to take the blame."

"It was your father's decision."

"But I consented."

I don't remember discussing the decision, and knowing my father, there probably was no discussion, only a decision, a lie, and a recitation. I don't remember clearly the run through the woods that night, only falling and feeling the wolf's breath against my neck. I do remember running into the house, into my father, who held my shoulders the way he held them on the day of my baptism when I walked into the river.

"You consented," she agrees, and looks at me levelly. "Your father sacrificed him, and you and your mother went along with it."

We look at Lyric, restless in her car seat, kicking her sandaled foot. Jewel pauses, holding the driver's side door. "You were just a girl then, Rachel. But then you weren't a girl anymore, and you kept on lying. The week before Garland died, I went to pick him up at a drug house early one Sunday morning. He didn't touch the stuff, but it had been a rare night out with a couple of high school friends, and they'd ended up at this place, out on 32. It's called Diamond City, I guess because that's where people go to get crushed. Anyway, I walked into this house, and there were people passed out, on the floors and tables, just bodies everywhere. And I thought the most integrated place in Shiloh is a drug house on Sunday morning. Black and white and brown, lying together, high as kites and dead to the world. There, in the center, was Garland, sober and still as a mouse. He cried without making a sound all the way home. I asked him what was wrong, what was going on, but he wouldn't say. I think he envied their oblivion, and he wanted a more permanent darkness. Ten days later I found out I was pregnant. I called him, but he was already dead."

HOURS LATER I'M in the deer stand sulking like a child. I pace and jab at the air. All I've done is to return to a place I couldn't be bothered to visit when it mattered, when my family was living.

Arguing uselessly, silently, with myself, I go for a drive, taking the long way around town, six miles instead of four, and stop in the church parking lot.

A few years after Professor's death, I had asked Minister Swain questions that had begun to nag at me, about the existence of heaven and hell, and how the saved could bear eternal life given the eternal suffering of the damned. The thing to remember, Minister Swain said, is that God wants us all to be saved. He might, I replied, but Miss Leota doesn't. He laughed and said, I'll remind Leota you can't get to heaven on other people's sins. I wore him out with my follow-up questions, and it was his good-natured unflappability, and flickers of humble uncertainty, that made me feel softer toward him even after I resented, then abandoned, what I had learned in his church.

I leave the car and drift inside, reading the prayer requests and announcements on the vestibule bulletin board. Rambo the ram has escaped his farm and was last seen licking a cow through a pasture fence three miles away. Low voices carry from the front of the church, and glancing toward the pulpit I see Ernest the barfly with Minister Swain and Roberta. I open the door to sneak back out, but Roberta calls to me.

"I was just loitering," I say, my hand on the door.

"Come join us," Roberta says.

"I saved you a seat," Ernest says, patting the pew. He looks pale, his complexion pasty, I notice as I make my way down the aisle toward them. "I came here to give confession," he says, "but the minister won't hear it."

Minister Swain smiles. "I told Rachel the same, I'm not a priest. Your confession is between you and God. You can speak to him directly."

I haven't seen either of them since my own public confession in this same room, but they welcome me as they always have.

"I was Catholic for a few minutes," Ernest explains.

"I'm sure you can find a priest, probably within an hour's drive."

"I'd rather say it on home soil," Ernest says, lifting his bony hands to grip the pew in front of him, where Minister Swain and Roberta sit, turned toward him with soft encouraging faces.

"I'm intruding," I say, and turn to go.

"I witnessed your confession," Ernest says. "You witness mine." He pats the pew again and I sit on the end, stiff and upright.

"It's those men I killed in the war," he begins immediately, without preamble. "So many men. Some of their faces I never saw and others were as close to me as you are," he says, and turns his head, looking at each of us. He inhales, swallows a whistle, examines his murderous hands. "I led ambushes, killed men every live-long day. My wife has been dead five years, but I can picture the faces of some of those dead boys from fifty years ago better than I can my own wife."

No one knows what to say, not even, it seems, Minister Swain, unless he is holding his tongue while Ernest unburdens his heart.

"See, we would go through the pockets of the dead after ambushes. Some carried pictures of wives or girlfriends, and we took them. Sometimes they were pictures of their own women and sometimes they were pictures of the wives and girlfriends of our soldiers. We knew they went through the pockets of our dead, too. It was seeing those pictures in their pockets, it made me crazy."

"What did you do with them?"

"Burned them."

The image is so sudden and powerful that I can almost taste ash in my mouth.

"I burned them and made a habit of it, a ritual really. I ought not to have done that. Now I'm not here at the end wishing everything could have been done different. But I do wish I hadn't burned those pictures. I still remember. I forget plenty, other things drop away, but those pictures are still here," he says, touching his temple, "in my mind. I burned those things and now they're burned into me. I'll never be rid of them."

Minister Swain comes around to our pew and I stand to let him in, but he ignores me, sliding in so that the three of us sit together, with me awkward in the middle. Roberta watches us from the pew ahead, our intercessor.

"You are rid of them," the minister says to Ernest. "Now you have to rid yourself of guilt. That's all that's left. Ask God for forgiveness and when he grants it, accept it."

I'm not sure what to do, so I cross my legs and look down at my hands in my lap.

"What would you like to do, Ernest?" Roberta asks, and I remember how she always said that to me and Professor— What would you like to do today?—and the world opened to us. Everyone else was too busy, except her. Minister Swain glances at his wife, and I wonder whether she's having a good day or Pick's disease isn't noticeable yet.

"What do I want to do?" Ernest asks quietly. "I want to put my affairs in order. And I just don't know what to do with these pictures in my mind."

He goes silent and we all look toward the pulpit, at the crucifixion hanging near the choir.

"Give it to God," Minister Swain says, and I stare at the tormented body on the wall while they close their eyes and pray.

AFTER ERNEST LEAVES, I sit with Roberta and Minister Swain. It's awkward but they make it less so. I killed their son and I need to do my time. When they offer to pray with me, I can't stand it anymore.

"Aren't you going to rebuke me?"

They look at me with scrutiny, but not fury or enmity or bitterness.

"We know," Roberta says, and I wonder if she means we *knew*. "Rufus has been dead thirty years. I loved him, and he loved you."

"We also know," Minister Swain continues, and for a

moment he averts his eyes and brings his hand to his face, "that you suffer, too."

Roberta takes my hand, and her kindness is my damnation. They're as modest and sincere as my own parents. They look at me piercingly and I try to meet their gaze.

"Are you planning to stay?" Roberta asks.

"Yes. For now."

"Good, good," Minister Swain says. "Roberta and I have been talking. You created a ripple at the meeting."

I nod, acknowledging this truth, and wonder what it means to live in a place where you cause ripples. I've always thought that was to be avoided, but it seems right that I should live here, where I'm challenged and confronted.

"I can see that you are used to teaching," he says carefully, and I suppose that is his polite way of saying I'm a pedantic asshole.

"What Jefferson is trying to say, Rachel, is we want to try to heal this rift, so that these conversations can continue, over time. We, too, want to take guns out of the hands of children. But maybe we should give people time to know you again, to trust you."

"So," Minister Swain continues, "we'd like to have a small gathering, to welcome you home. To share a meal, to talk, and not, well . . . *preach*."

"Do you think that's a good idea? We'll never agree on most things. And I don't mind keeping to myself. I've probably made a few enemies."

"I wouldn't say enemies, Rachel. These are your neighbors. It's a small community, and you're . . ." he stumbles and smiles.

"In a 'cloud of witnesses,'" Roberta says gently.

Minister Swain nods in agreement. "People here, like most people most places, find it hard to be criticized by one of their own."

One of their own? Am I deceiving them or myself?

"Would you agree to a small gathering, Rachel? We could have it here or—"

"Here?" I say in alarm. "Oh, no. I'll host it, at the farm."

"Are you sure? It can be a potluck. I'll bake a cake."

"Roberta, would you help me invite people? I don't have much experience with this."

"Of course. Choose a date, maybe a Saturday afternoon, and give me a call."

TWENTY-ONE

I WALK DOWN the hall, and finally open my parents' door. The room is still, the air stale. I open a window and a breeze lifts the curtains. Professor and I had gotten in trouble once for reenacting biblical scenes. I was Mary, washing the feet of a very tickly Jesus, who became tangled up in the curtains, and fell, pulling down his curtain shroud, and the curtain rod, too. I had been banned from playing in their room after that.

Garland had understood from the start that their room was off limits. I, however, had to be told outright this room was private, this room with its brown and green rugs and chenille bedspread. There is no art on the walls; no books on the night-stand; there is no nightstand. A bed, a dresser, a chair with a cane seat, supposedly made by some ancestor we never fully knew about. There were local stories sure, but genealogy, like travel and novels, were for people of a different class, peo-ple with leisure time for leisure activities. My parents had no time for leisure, and, if they had had the *time*, they still would have had no *time* for it. They were always occupied with farm work, though they were never hurried or harried, not in any visible way.

I have to put this house in order, in my mother's words. She was not chatty, considering too many words frivolous, or, worse, wasteful. Waste was her prince of darkness. My father's, too. He carried nothing in his pockets but his knife, which he wielded like a worn key, with ease and skill and a sense of proportion.

I kneel by their bed and try to pray, to say a secular prayer. I take the shoebox from under the bed and wander the halls. In the kitchen, I tape the torn picture of me and Garland and the gun rack above the phone, and call Tobias.

"Do you think you could find a day to go to the ocean with me?"

"To the Sand Dollar?" he says, and I wonder if it's impulsive or something he's thought of proposing and decided not to. "Are you asking me on a date?"

"Sure, but my parents will be with us."

He laughs quietly, digesting my response. "Wait. What?"

"I want to scatter their ashes in the Atlantic. I can do it alone, but I have to rent a boat. You have to be three miles from shore, and I get seasick. I wouldn't mind the company."

"Are you inviting me to hold your barf bag?"

"I'll hold it, but I might have to hand you the ashes while I use it."

"Since you've made it sound so appealing, I wouldn't mind the excursion."

"Good. I'll book the boat."

TWENTY-TWO

WHEN I FIRST moved to New York, I had imagined myself at literary parties, discussing books and indulging in the sad jokes of English majors the world over. But there had been very few parties. Today, I pause to feel the breeze through the screen and take a minute to marvel at the party on the lawn, this strange assemblage of locals.

As I come outside with silverware, they stand vivid in the bright light—Jewel and Lyric and Palmer; Tom and Tobias; the minister and Roberta; Billy from the bar; shy Annie with flowers in her hair, who is singing to the crowd; Dennis and Ernest standing slightly apart, passing a flask; and Eva, the evil postmistress, watching her sad alcoholic husband and two tan, bug-bitten children. Shep the warden has taken a plate and is eyeing the grill. Pearl and Vasta are talking with Tilly, who I know came for Tom. Burl has left them and moved to Greenvale, and she is watching Tom protectively, her left hand crossed over her right, forcing herself not to rush to his side.

I'm surprised at how fond I've grown of this group, in this place that is a paradox. Judgment and redemption; history and myth; punishment and atonement: Shiloh is my Wilderness.

Roberta comes to help, looking thin and polite, and insisting on taking napkins from my hand.

"I was just thinking how Rufus said he was going to marry you."

"Maybe I'm waiting for him. I'm still available." We were eight years old when he proposed. I had let him kiss me, had instructed him, really, after I broke the handle of the vanity mirror I had previously used for practice.

She stops and puts her hand on my arm. "But you're not available, are you Rachel? You're not available at all."

"I suppose not, but I'm trying."

"Don't think you can change the past," she says, as we continue across the yard. "But you can change your life."

"I don't want to cause you more pain. Do I constantly remind you of him?"

"Nothing disturbs my memories of Rufus. If that's what's worrying you, put it out of your mind. Don't turn away from all you might see in this world, even right here, in our little town."

As we join the others, she looks at me, not with slyness exactly, but with a knowingness that gives me the strangest feeling of being restored and perhaps even blessed.

THE LAND LUMPS us together, like it or not. We are joined: for all of us here, the boundaries are porous between past and present, dead and living; they all lean on one another, like the language itself, no separation, only one long, pauseless sentence. That's what I love about it. I hate it, too. That's why I want to keep it close, so I can hate it better. Know thy enemy, as thyself.

What's left for me in New York anyway? Years of solitary struggle, of passively consuming a culture I'm not contributing to. In my last meeting with the department chair, who was just returning from a conference at one of the better public universities, I asked her how her panel was, in an excruciating effort at small talk. She sighed, and said, "Well, you know, we have to do these things sometimes. But it was just a big gathering of have-nots."

I look at my gathering of have-nots. I may as well cast my lot here, with a new start in an old place. I am a caretaker, only a groundsperson, and will try to remember that.

Tobias and Tom are whispering and gently slapping each other on the arm. I hear my name, and they come over.

"What are you two in cahoots about?"

"We've found you a horse."

"I don't need a horse."

"Yes, you do. You need a horse so June won't get spoiled."

I look over at June, who is eating corn off the cob Jewel is holding for her.

"I don't know anything about horses or how to care for them."

"That's where Tom comes in. He has agreed to help you."

Tom looks at me with pleading eyes.

"I'll think about it. Don't get your hopes up."

Taking Tobias aside, I tell him I'll consider housing a horse if he will help me change crops. I tell him I'm thinking of lavender and sweet potatoes. He starts to protest, saying it requires infrastructure and investment, but I cut him off. I tell him I've researched it, and I've signed up for the state erosion prevention program, which is giving a bonus and annual payments in exchange for an agreement not to cut timber from the surrounding woods for twenty years.

"But we're sixty miles from water!" Tobias says. "What erosion?"

"Doesn't matter. We're in one of the counties covered by the program. I've already talked to their office. A lawyer is coming out Monday."

"That won't be enough to live on."

"I've got enough for now, all in all."

"It's not easy to change crops. It's a lot of labor."

"That's fine."

"It's hard, Rachel, it's backbreaking, it's not—"

"I have an inheritance, and I have to steward the land as best I can."

"Still stubborn as a mule."

"Mules are underrated. We'll start small and see how it goes."

"You are the most hard-headed person I've ever met."

"My skull is the same as everyone else's."

DENNIS PASSES ME a plate with pork, roasted corn, and Eva's slaw. As I'm contemplating the meat and wondering about its origins, Ernest leans over.

"I selected that pig. You don't trust it?"

"It's not that. I was just thinking," I say, stalling, "about where it came from."

"You eat that pig. He lived right down the road, and had a good life on a small farm. Hell, Rachel, that pig and I enjoyed roughly the same circle of friends."

The others cluster around, and we laugh and eat and talk about coyotes and the price of corn and how to get rid of hornworms and what will really replace tobacco.

Dennis is introduced to Shep and asks him if he's ever seen a red wolf. Shep tells about a woman in a neighboring county who tried to mail what she said was a rug. The rug was leaking blood from the shipping box, and when the police were called, they found a red wolf hide.

"So they do exist," Ernest says.

"Unless the last one was in a box to Canada for tanning."

The sound of laughter is carried on the breeze as I look at Lyric and whisper her name. Miraculously, she looks across the distance and gives me a smile and a fist pump.

"I love her, Jewel," I blurt.

"You look stricken, and also like Garland. It's your mouth, the way you pull it down on the left side."

"I do. I've never said that before."

"What?"

"I've never in my life said 'I love you' to anyone."

"You can't be serious."

"I am." I shake my head. Maybe it hasn't been entirely absent from my life, but it has always been absent from my vocabulary.

She looks at me, searching, then a smile spreads and she laughs. "I can see you mean it. Well, you're about to get a real education."

I'm almost giddy, ridiculous.

"The book club has doubled," Vasta says, handing me a napkin and pointing to my chin. "Jewel has agreed to join as long as we let her choose the next book and work with her schedule."

"And Lyric?"

"I thought Tom might agree to babysit for a small fee. We'll be right there in the next room."

"That's the best idea I've heard in ages."

At eight the sheriff arrives. He's a solid man with a heavy jaw and lines fanning from his eyes. We haven't spoken since Garland's death and neither of us mentions it now. He doesn't truck in small talk, and tells me he's here to collect the guns I called to turn in: Vasta's pistol, the inherited collection I asked Tobias to store.

Jewel puts Lyric in my arms and unwraps Garland's last gun from a satin pillowcase. "This one, too," she says, picking it up with two fingers and setting it carefully on the ground. The sheriff moves with skill, making sure they're all unloaded and placing them in his trunk.

"We might round up a few more."

"Let's not start a trend," he says.

TWENTY-THREE

I AM IN a deep sleep and someone is calling my name from far
away. I lie paralyzed, between dream and waking. Someone is
in distress. Someone is in pain. A hand moves toward my face,
and I realize it is my own.

"Rachel!"

I rise from the couch like a specter, and go to the door.

"Rachel! Come!"

He's standing in the dark behind the screen, his white
T-shirt glowing in the dark.

"Professor?"

I slide the screen door open and step into the night. It is
entirely soundless as I move toward the boy I killed.

"It's Tom. Can you come? There's something hurt in the
woods."

"Tom, how did you get here? It's two a.m."

"My bike. I snuck out," he says, and my heart freezes.

"Let me give you a ride home. We'll go to the woods in the
morning."

In the dark, he reaches for my hand.

"No. Come."

I am still waking as I grab a flashlight, stomp into my shoes, and follow. I try to ask again what's in the woods, but Tom walks fast down the drive, past his bike, and at the road, he breaks into a run.

It is full dark, and I jog sleepily behind him. He picks up the pace, and I follow. We are in flight now, fleeing, and it is that night again:

Run!

I look up at the stars in their measureless space, and time collapses and Garland is ahead of me and Professor is behind and a strange sound comes from my throat and it is almost a sigh but becomes a hiccup.

"Here!" Tom says, and stops beside the ditch, holding out his hand to me.

I take his warm child's hand and we jump the ditch together.

"What is it?"

"You'll see."

I look up at the starry sky and think the stars starring and the bodies fleeing are the same everywhere. There is motion there is distance there is death.

"Come!" he demands, and I follow.

I am fully awake now, shining the flashlight at our feet. It's that night again, and this time I am unarmed, totally defenseless.

"Here," he says. We are at Big Beech Island. A deer, a white doe, lies on her side. The flashlight catches the terror in her eyes.

"Oh, Tom."

"We have to save her."

I put my hand over his on the flashlight and guide it down

the doe's body. Her flank is bloody, and her left leg is crooked, as though pointing in accusation.

"Let's drag her out. We'll put her in your car and drive her to the vet."

"That won't help her, Tom. She's not going to make it."

"Why is she white?"

"She's missing pigment. There's a word for it, leucism. I've heard about them, but I've never seen one."

The doe gazes at us, unable to run, her pink tongue between her lips laboring at dying. She trembles and makes a low sound of mourning. Tom touches her head. She tries to back away, but he keeps stroking her between the ears, speaking in a soft, comforting voice.

"Why all the good ones?" he asks, as though questioning a child. "Why all the best ones got to go?"

The doe shudders.

"You're comforting her, Tom. She knows you're here."

The doe is not moving and Tom leans down, nuzzling her throat.

"Pretty doe." He is crying in her neck now and she does not move, but looks at me with the sibylline eyes of a deer learning the mysteries of death. I do not know how to comfort either of them.

"Deer were here before us," I find myself saying uselessly. "You're with her, Tom. She's not alone."

"We have to bury her."

"Should we get Tobias to help?"

"No. Just us."

WE RETURN TO the house for a sheet and a shovel. We take turns digging; he won't let me do it alone. As we are digging,

I lift the flashlight and catch a pair of eyes. If it is the wolf, he could easily take the doe from us, but he does not.

We drag the doe into the hole. Tom cries, "Wait!" and unclips Lily's stuffed horse from his jeans belt loop. He gently drops it on top of the doe.

"Are you sure, Tom?"

"I'm sure."

As we leave a light wind rises. The trees creak and groan and the ghosts are with us, guiding us. I keep my hand on Tom's shoulder, and he does not shake me off.

I PUT HIS bike in the trunk and drive him home. He tells me he has snuck out of the house and his mother doesn't know he's gone. But when we drive up, she is on the porch, pacing.

"Tom?" she says, "where have you been? I didn't know you were gone. I just came out to get some air."

"I rode my bike," he says. "I couldn't sleep."

He disappears inside the house, and I try to explain to Tilly that we both had something to put to rest.

"Is he going to be all right?" Tilly asks.

"He's suffering. He'll learn to live with it."

"We all—" She nods, covering her mouth and turning away.

AT HOME, I visit my ghostless, batless attic. It's as though I'm visiting myself, opening the final room in the house I built in my head. So here I find you, old sinner, the hunter says to the wolf in the story. Here I find you, I say to myself in the attic. Here I am.

June stays downstairs, on her cushion, pretending to guard the house. I appreciate this time to commune with my ghostly self. I lie down on the floor, knees up, arms out. *Oh, I was so frightened! Red Riding Hood tells the hunter.* I turn my head and see her, my younger self, running full speed toward the house while Professor lay dying. *It was so dark inside the wolf's body!*

That terrified girl, that murderous self, finally lets go as I lie still. It is a strange sensation, as though a shadow body is lifting, separating, from my belly button to my collarbone. Then a moving away, and I am light and wonderfully empty.

June comes up and circles around before clicking back downstairs to find her outline in the couch cushion. First, she checks on me, leaning over to lick my face. I think of telling her there's a reason witches prefer cats. But June and I understand one another perfectly.

I sleep alone on the attic floor, safe and light as the witch who slips her skin. There is no one to prevent me. I *am* the witch slipping my skin.

In the morning, I return to my body, and descend the attic stairs refreshed. June and I sally out as the sun rises.